STICK DOG COMES TO TOWN

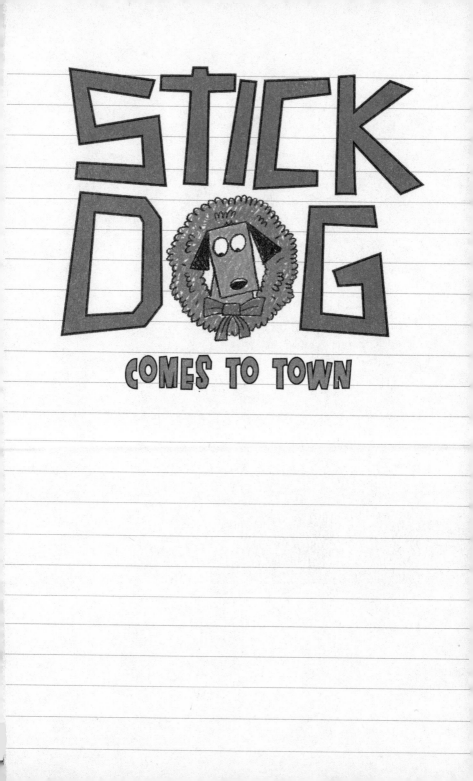

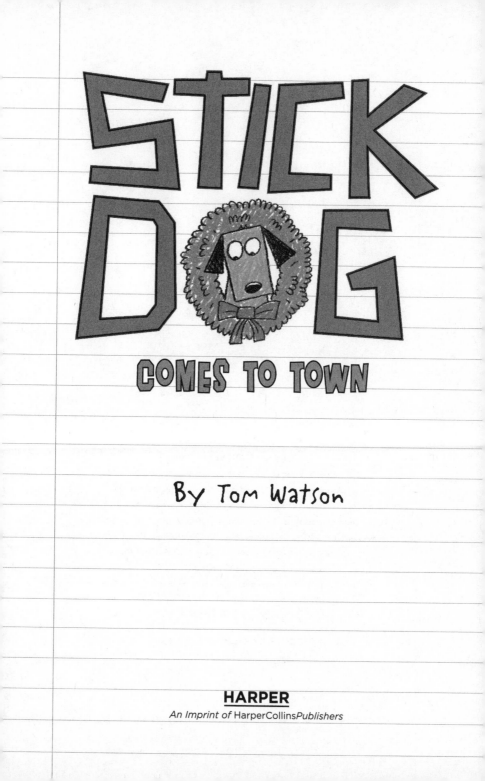

STICK DOG

COMES TO TOWN

By Tom Watson

HARPER
An Imprint of HarperCollinsPublishers

Library of Congress Control Number: 2021939625

ISBN 978-0-06-301422-0

21 22 23 24 25   PC/LSCH   10 9 8 7 6 5 4 3 2 1

❖

First Edition

To: MEJ
(YGATB)

TABLE OF CONTENTS

Chapter 1

MUTT'S SHOE COLLECTION

Mutt was on the old couch cushion in Stick Dog's pipe below Highway 16. He was surrounded by shoes. He had recently discovered that shoes were his new and absolute favorite things to chew on. So whenever the dogs were out and about searching for food, they searched for shoes for Mutt too.

They had collected more than a dozen so far. They found shoes in garbage cans that Poo-Poo knocked over by ramming headfirst into them. They found shoes at Picasso Park, on the side of the road, and lots of places.

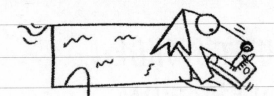

Mutt chewed on a blue basketball sneaker
at this particular moment.

"How's the shoe, Mutt?" Stripes asked. She
and Poo-Poo sat side by side to stay warm.
It was winter.

"It's fantastic," Mutt said after dropping the
shoe from his mouth. He didn't want to be
impolite. "Just fantastic."

"What's fantastic about it?" Poo-Poo asked.
He wasn't making fun; he was curious.
"Why's it better than chewing on a Frisbee?
Or a mitten or something?"

"It's a great question," Mutt answered. "You see, with a shoe it's just the entire chewing experience. It's such a complete thing."

Stripes asked, "How so?"

"Shoes have different materials and textures and parts," Mutt explained. "The soles are usually soft and rubbery—a real relaxed and rhythmic chewing experience. The heels on fancy shoes can be hard, which is great for gnawing. And leather shoes are great for shredding. And I haven't even told you about the best part."

"What's the best part?" asked Poo-Poo.

"Shoestrings," Mutt said. "When I chew a shoestring, it often gets between my teeth.

I can pull it back and forth. It's a very satisfying feeling."

Poo-Poo and Stripes nodded their understanding, and Mutt got that sneaker back in his mouth. He went after the shoestrings first.

Stick Dog smiled. He had been listening to his friends' conversation from where he stood at the entrance to his pipe, staring out at the meadow and forest. There was a five-inch-thick layer of snow on the ground.

So far, it had been a gray day—for a couple of reasons.

It was cloudy—that was the first reason.

But they had also been unsuccessful in their search for food in the morning. The garbage cans at Picasso Park were all empty. It had been too busy in town to stop by Mike's Magnificent Meats to see their friend, Lucy—and see if she could sneak them some meaty scraps. Stick Dog had never seen so many humans bustling around the town's shops.

Their unsuccessful food search had made the gray day even grayer.

Then, around noon, everything brightened.

It started to snow—the very first snowfall of winter. And Stick Dog felt his spirits lift. The day felt just a little less gray. It was still cold—and he and his friends were still hungry. But there was something about the fresh snowfall that seemed to bring a magical brightness to the day.

And now, Stick Dog thought it seemed especially true. It was dusk. The remaining sunlight painted the sky in gold and pink. And the snow all around him glittered and reflected those bright colors.

Stick Dog was content to stand there—cold as he was—and watch how the day shifted into evening. He would have stayed there, no doubt, for several more minutes if someone didn't suddenly race out of the forest and across the meadow.

It was Karen, the dachshund.

And she had some news—startling news.

Chapter 2

A MAGIC TREE

Karen hustled into the pipe, slipping and sliding to a stop.

"I found a magic tree!" she exclaimed, breathing hard.

"A magic tree?" Stick Dog asked. You could tell by the tone of his voice that he didn't

believe in magic trees. But you could also tell
he was curious about what Karen thought
she had found.

"That's right," answered Karen immediately.
Her little dachshund body vibrated with
energy and glee. A fine mist of melted snow
sprang forth from her fur every time she
shook. "Magic."

"There's no such thing as
magic, Karen," Poo-Poo said.

"What about that one time
I caught my tail? January sixteenth!" Karen
said quickly. "That was the most magical day
of my life!"

Stick Dog didn't want the conversation
to devolve into the existence—or

nonexistence—of magic. He quickly refocused the subject.

“Karen,” he said. “Why don’t you tell us how you discovered this tree?”

She nodded her head with incredible vigor and began her story.

“I went to Fountain Square to get a drink,” Karen began.

Karen’s friends all knew exactly where she meant. There was a small square on Main Street in the nearby town. In the middle of the square was a fountain where the dogs had gotten fresh

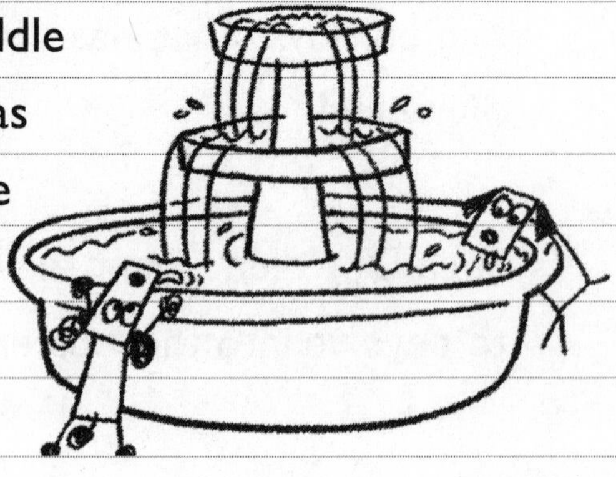

water to drink many times at night when no humans were around. It was close to Mike's, the store where their friend, Lucy, lived.

"I was really thirsty—and that fountain always has nice water," Karen continued. She looked around to make sure everybody else was listening. She liked being the center of attention like this. "Well, when I got there the water was totally frozen solid, which was a bummer."

Stick Dog didn't mention that the fountain had likely been frozen for at least a month. Instead, he said. "That's too bad. What happened next?"

"I heard a siren," Karen answered. "And I remembered what you always say, Stick Dog."

"I've always said that when we hear a siren, we should hide," Stick Dog said. "In case it's the dogcatcher or something. So, I bet you left that fountain and hid somewhere."

"That's exactly what I did!" Karen exclaimed. "I heard the siren and ran to hide under a big pine tree that was close to the fountain."

"Tell us all about it," encouraged Stick Dog.

"Okay, I will!" Karen went on enthusiastically. "Did you know that near pine tree trunks there's a nice open space?!"

"I did know that," Stick Dog answered. "Pine trees make great hiding spots because the branches hang down so low at the bottom."

"Right, right," Karen said. "Well, I was under that tree waiting for that siren to go away. It only took a few seconds. So I started out of that hiding place to get a drink of water from the fountain. I was still really thirsty."

Stick Dog said, "I thought you said the water in the fountain was frozen."

"That's right. I did say that."

"So, umm, did you search for water someplace else?" asked Stick Dog.

"Why in the world would I do that?" Karen replied. "When the fountain was right there?"

"But you knew the water in the fountain was frozen."

"I knew the water was frozen before I hid under the pine tree," Karen explained. "I didn't know it would be frozen after I stopped hiding."

"Oh, umm, okay," Stick Dog said, resisting the urge to smack a paw against his forehead. "And how long were you hiding?"

"I'd say about fifteen seconds or so."

ICE CUBE → 15 SECONDS → PUDDLE

"And you thought the ice in the fountain might have melted in that fifteen seconds?"

"Sure," Karen said with happiness and innocence in her voice. "I'm a believer, Stick Dog. I like to surround myself with tons of positive energy and believe that awesome things can happen. That's one of the things that makes me special!"

Stick Dog couldn't help it. He had to smile.

"You are quite special, that is for certain," he said. "So did the ice melt?"

"I don't know."

"Why not."

"I never made it back to the fountain."

"You didn't?"

"No."

"Why not?"

"Because that's when the magic happened!"

"How did the magic happen?"

"I hit my head! Isn't that wonderful?!"

Chapter 3

PINE CONES ARE DELICIOUS

"Hitting your head was the magic part, Karen?" Stick Dog asked.

"That's right!" she answered, pointing at the top of her head.

"Karen," Poo-Poo interjected. He seemed compelled to speak. He was, as you know, quite an expert on this subject. "I've hit my head into hundreds of things. I've bashed into tree trunks, big rocks, garbage cans, swing sets—all kinds of stuff. The pain is quite intense sometimes. Of course, the relief I feel when the pain goes away afterward is just as strong. That's why I do it—to feel that great sense of relief. It's awesome. But I wouldn't call it *magical*."

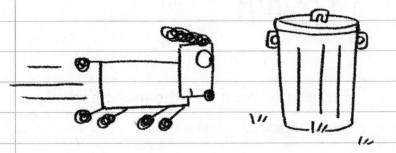

"Thanks for that unique insight, Poo-Poo," Stick Dog said, and then turned to Karen. "I guess we'd all like to understand how hitting your head was magical."

"Well, it wasn't the actual hitting of my head," Karen revealed. "It's what I hit my head into!"

"And what was that?" asked Stripes.

"It was the strangest pine cone I've ever seen!" Karen exclaimed. "That's what made that pine tree a magic tree. It was covered in magic pine cones!"

The entire group—even Stick Dog—found this fascinating. They stepped even closer, forming a tight circle around her. Karen spun slowly there as she provided more and more information.

"The pine cones were not shaped like pine cones at all."

Stripes asked, "What shape were these magic pine cones?"

"They were long and skinny—with hooks on one end. Like a curve."

Mutt asked, "What color were these long, thin, hooked, magic pine cones?"

"They weren't brown like regular pine cones," Karen answered, her eyes stretched wide. "They were red and white and sort of, like, striped!"

Poo-Poo asked, "How many of these long, thin, hooked, red-and-white-striped, magic pine cones were there?"

"Hundreds and hundreds!" Karen yelled.

"Karen," Stick Dog said calmly. "How were these, umm, magic pine cones in the tree?"

"They hung on the tree—just like regular pine cones."

"Fascinating," Stick Dog said, more to himself than to his friends. Karen's description was so specific and detailed that he had little doubt that she had actually discovered something. He didn't suspect that they were actually, you know, magical. But he was certainly interested in finding out more about the objects that Karen described. Next time they were in town and close to the fountain, he would like to investigate that tree.

But there was still something Stick Dog didn't know. And that something would make him change his mind quickly about investigating that tree sometime in the future.

Karen wasn't all the way done with her description yet. She had left out the most important detail.

She had saved the best for last.

"There's one more thing," Karen said in a quieter, more dramatic voice. "It's the most magical thing of all!"

"What?!?!" Stripes, Mutt, and Poo-Poo screamed in unison.

"Those magic pine cones," Karen began, and paused. She lifted one eyebrow and grinned from the corner of her mouth. It was certainly evident that she liked building up the suspense of the moment. "Are delicious! I licked one!"

Mutt, Poo-Poo, and Stripes stared at Karen.
They couldn't believe what she just said.

They all knew, after all, that you can't eat
pine cones.

Then the four of them jerked their heads
toward Stick Dog.

He said just one thing.

"Let's go!"

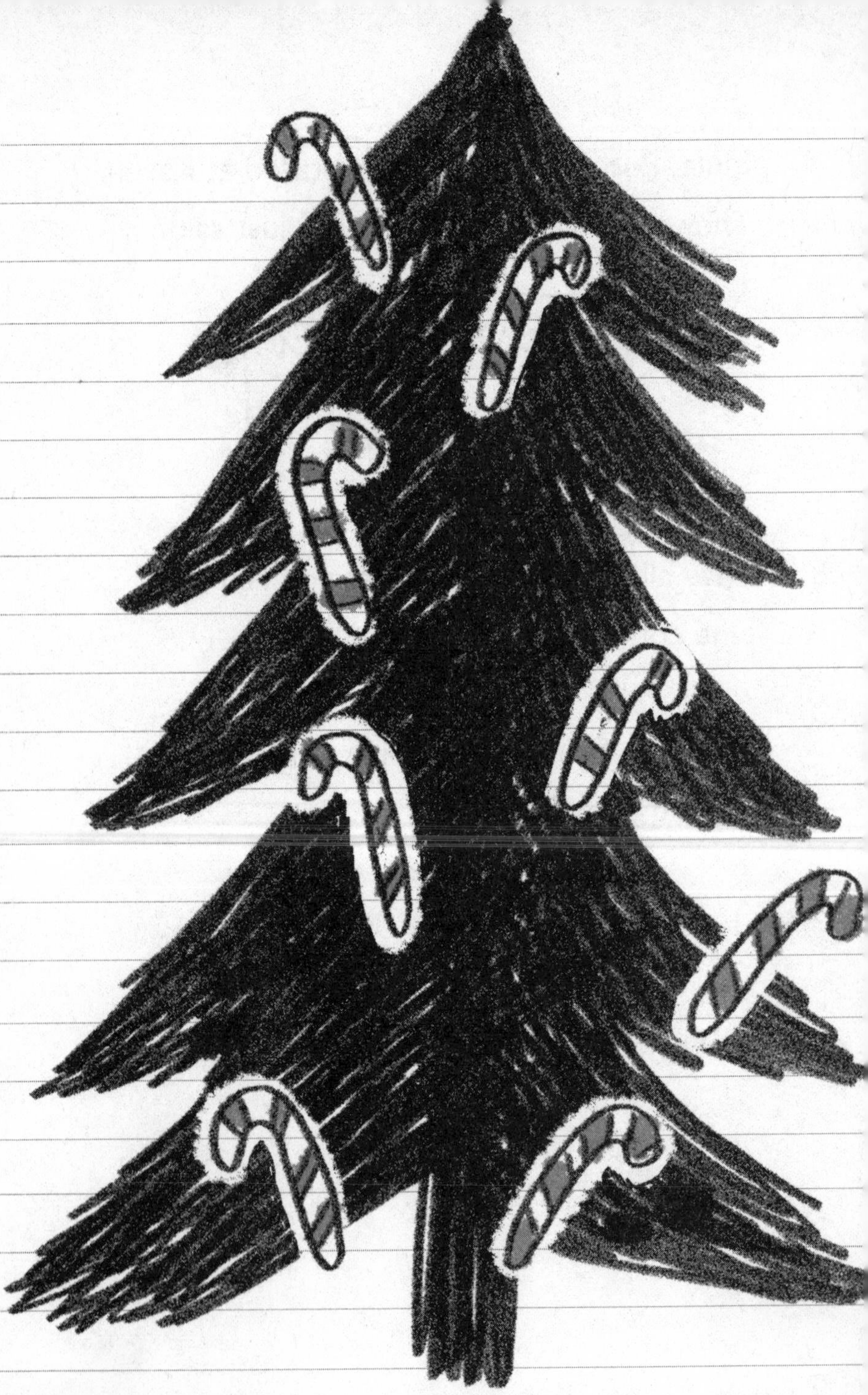

Chapter 4

SWEET AND MINTY

It didn't take long for the five dogs to reach Fountain Square. Once they got to the edge of town, they scurried and skittered around parked cars, garbage cans, and benches. They stayed safely hidden from the few humans who were around.

They snuck their way to Fountain Square in three minutes.

And they saw the huge pine tree.

It was exactly as Karen had described. It was big. It was close to the fountain. And it was covered with lots and lots of those magical pine cones that she was so excited about.

Stick Dog stuck his head out from the left side of a bench and looked left and right. He looked left and right again. There were no humans very close. He thought they could make it without being seen.

"Okay," he said, turning back to his friends. "We're going to do exactly what Karen did earlier. We'll duck under those low-hanging branches of the pine tree and hide by the trunk. Then we'll check out the red and white things."

"Stick Dog?" Karen asked.

"Yes?"

"I'm going to stop by the fountain on the way to get a drink of water," she said. "I'm still thirsty."

"The water is frozen, Karen," he said quickly. "You can't drink it."

"How do you know that?" Karen asked.

"Because you were there earlier tonight and it was frozen then," Stick Dog said. He didn't want to get into this now—not while the coast was clear. "Just eat some snow. That will relieve your thirst. That's what we always do in the winter."

"Oh, Stick Dog, Stick Dog," Stripes said. She seemed to be talking on Karen's behalf. "She's not hungry, she's thirsty. She doesn't want to eat something. She wants to drink something."

Mutt and Poo-Poo seemed to rally to this way of thinking. They nodded their heads in agreement and chimed in with their own comments.

Poo-Poo said, "You can only drink liquids, Stick Dog. Everybody knows that."

Mutt added, "Snow is not a liquid."

Stick Dog closed his eyes and took a deep, calming breath. He pictured the trees outside his pipe from earlier—when winter's first snowfall began to cover their branches in a soft, glistening white. He exhaled slowly, opened his eyes, and responded to his friends.

"You're all correct about everything, of course," Stick Dog said. "But I think we've talked about this before. In fact, I seem to remember talking about this very subject at the beginning of every winter."

"Talk about what?" Karen asked.

"How snow is kind of like frozen rain," Stick Dog began to explain. He did his best to remember what he told his friends at the first snowfall the previous year. And the year before that. And the year before that. And, you know, all the years before that. "If you get some snow in your mouth it will melt very quickly and turn into water."

"But we need to drink a liquid, Stick Dog," Poo-Poo argued. "A liquid."

"Water, umm, is a liquid," Stick Dog whispered slowly.

"Oh, right."

Stick Dog decided to stop talking. Instead, he leaned down and took a big bite of snow from the ground. He lifted his head, squeezed his lips together, and allowed the snow to melt in his mouth. It only took a couple of

seconds. Then he swallowed as loudly and deliberately as he could.

This was all Karen, Poo-Poo, Mutt, and Stripes needed to see. All four of them quickly plunged their muzzles into the snow, took some bites, waited for it to melt into water, and then swallowed. They did this several times each.

"Well, how about that?" Mutt said. "It really does work. Thanks for telling us about it, Stick Dog."

"No problem," he replied. He eyeballed the route from the bench to the big pine tree and deemed it safe again. "Come on!"

Stick Dog raced out from behind the bench and crossed the snow-covered square—passing by the fountain as he did. When he reached the big pine tree, he skidded to a stop. He lifted one of the lower branches into the air and all the other dogs ducked beneath.

There was not a ton of room underneath the tree, but there was enough for them to settle in.

"Do you think we're safe in here, Stick Dog?" Stripes asked.

"I think so, yes," Stick Dog answered as he looked around. "I don't think a human could ever see us through this tree's thick branches. And I highly doubt any human will come in here. It's even a little warmer in here with the branches and pine needles blocking the wind. It's nice."

These assurances from Stick Dog helped everyone relax.

"Then what do we do now?" Mutt asked.

Stick Dog didn't hesitate to answer.

"I think we should try these red and white things," he said. "Right now."

"They're not things, Stick Dog," Karen corrected. "They're pine cones. Magic pine cones."

"If you say so, Karen," Stick Dog answered quickly. "Magic pine cones it is."

The red and white objects were more difficult to see from inside the tree than from outside. But it took less than a minute for each of the dogs to catch a glimpse of those colors among the dark green pine needles. They each plucked one off.

Poo-Poo sniffed at it.

"There is something strangely familiar about this scent," Poo-Poo declared. He was the group's foremost authority on flavors and aromas. He lifted his chin in the air slightly and continued. "I'm reminded of two things as I contemplate this smell."

"What two things, Poo-Poo?" Mutt asked.

"First, I'm reminded of the wild mint that grows near the creek in springtime," Poo-Poo answered. They all knew that smell. In the first weeks of spring, clumps of mint leaves blossomed near the creek where they usually got their water. It was a delicious smell. "Secondly, I recall that strange, strange night a couple of years ago."

"What night, Poo-Poo?" Stripes asked.

"That night we saw those two witches and got all that candy," Poo-Poo replied, nodding his head. He talked faster now, getting excited. "That's it, all right. That's it exactly! This aroma is sugary and sweet! And minty!"

They didn't need to hear anything else—

and they certainly didn't need to wait any longer. All five dogs began to lick those magic pine cones.

They licked them slowly at first, just with the tips of their tongues. But that didn't last long. Soon they were lapping at them as fully and furiously as they could. That only lasted another minute though.

Soon they realized that they could also bite these newly discovered objects. They were crunchy, a little bit sticky—and sugary and minty.

Scrumptious.

As soon as they finished one delicious

treat, they snatched another from the pine tree's dark green branches and needles. This process—licking, biting, chewing, finishing, and grabbing another—went on for a good ten minutes, maybe longer.

And while that was going on inside the tree, something else was going on outside the tree.

Stick Dog didn't realize it until something dangerous happened.

As he lay on his belly licking another red and white treat, something suddenly plunged through the tree right at his head.

It was a human hand.

Chapter 5

WAIT A MINUTE

Stick Dog jerked back from that human hand as quickly as he could. He was completely surprised—and totally startled. His sudden movement caught the instant attention of Poo-Poo, Stripes, Karen, and Mutt. They held perfectly still.

"Be absolutely quiet!" Stick Dog scream-whispered.

Now that his heart had settled a little bit, Stick Dog could see that this was a little human's hand.

And it wasn't trying to grab him at all.

It was trying to reach one of the red and white magic pine cones.

"Candy cane!" a tiny female human's voice yelled from outside the tree. That hand searched all around—and almost brushed against Stick Dog's left cheek. He caught a glimpse of red and white from the corner of his eye. He reached out with his front left paw very slowly, grasped the magic pine cone, and pushed it toward the little human's tiny fingers. She grabbed it. "Got one!"

And just as fast as her little hand had plunged into the tree—it jerked back out just as quickly.

"I'm glad you got one," an older human voice nearby said. "Come over here. It's almost time to start."

Stick Dog breathed a quiet sigh and turned to his friends.

"It's okay," he whispered. He held up his red and white treat, pointed at it, and added, "They're called candy canes."

There was something about learning that name, feeling safe again, and being out of reach of that human hand that washed over Stick Dog then. He was relieved. Relaxed. Secure. Happy.

He looked at his friends. Mutt, Karen, Poo-Poo, and Stripes had all taken their cue from him. They were relaxed and happy too—and returned their full attention to their candy canes.

Stick Dog liked to see them like that. He enjoyed watching them.

For seven seconds.

After seven seconds, something occurred to him.

"Wait a minute," he whispered to himself. He tilted his head to the left and squinted his right eye halfway shut. It was getting late and cold. It was certainly dark. There weren't even very many big humans out a little while ago. "What is that little human doing here?

What's going on?"

Stick Dog put his candy cane down on the ground next to him, dropped to his belly, and scooched very slowly away from the tree trunk. He kept his head low and pushed through one of those low-hanging branches that brushed against the ground. He didn't go very far out.

Not very far at all.

Just the tip of his nose.

But it was enough for him to see.

He saw a little female human there. He recognized her hand—and that candy cane she was licking. Her parents were with her.

And so were some other humans. A whole lot of humans. They were gathered all around that tree.

Stick Dog knew one thing for sure.

There was no way to get out.

They were trapped.

Chapter 6

THERE'S A BANANA IN YOUR EAR

Stick Dog scooted back on his belly, returning to his friends in that open space near the tree trunk.

He didn't know what was happening outside that big pine tree, but he felt pretty safe. Those humans could not see them—he was positive about that. And it was cold and late at night. He didn't think they would be out there very long.

"Hey, everybody," Stick Dog whispered. He didn't want his friends to be alarmed, but definitely wanted to warn them about the humans. He certainly didn't want them to yelp real loud or for Karen to rush out to try to get a drink from the frozen water fountain. "I need to tell you something."

"What is it, Stick Dog?" Mutt whispered back after taking his candy cane from his mouth. He was very polite that way. "What can we do for you?"

Sorry, I need to interrupt here for a second. This won't take long. I want to see what happens here too. I mean, why are those people gathering around that tree? We'll find out in a minute. But the way Mutt responded here made me think of something.

Isn't it weird how if you whisper to someone they almost always whisper back? It's totally true. Have you ever noticed that? It's like if you start with a whisper, then there's something secret going on. Or there's a mystery. Or danger. Whatever it is, it's whisper-important.

You can test it out with an experiment.

Wait until you're somewhere with several people around. You know, the grocery store or the school hallway or the playground or somewhere. For this hypothetical and super-scientific example, let's say you're at the grocery store with your dad. Here's how you can test it.

"Dad?" you whisper to him.

"Yes?" he'll whisper back. "What is it?"

See how that worked?! He whispered because you whispered! And the whole conversation continues in whispers.

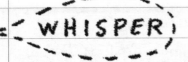

"There's a banana in your ear," you whisper.

Then your dad's eyes dart to the left and right, trying to see that banana from the

corner of his eye. Then he asks in a whisper,
"Which ear?"

"Your left ear."

"I don't remember putting a banana in my
ear. Why would I do that?"

There's really not a banana in your
dad's ear, of course. That's not what the
experiment is about. It's about whispering.

Now, I know what you're
going to say. You're going
to say, "But what if my
dad really does have a
banana in his ear?"

Well, then it doesn't work. Because there's
no secrecy or mystery. The super-scientific

experiment fails. The conversation would just be different. It would go something like this.

"Dad?" you whisper to him.

"Yes," he'll whisper back. "What is it?"

(See?! Still whispering!)

"There's a banana in your ear."

"Of course there's a banana in my ear," he'll say in a regular voice now because there's no more mystery or secrecy. "I'm surprised you didn't notice it before. I put it in there a couple of days ago. I'm waiting for it to get ripe. It was still a bit green. I like my bananas to be a little more yellow."

So, if your dad does have a banana in his

ear and you want to try out this whole whisper-experiment thing, you need to come up with something else instead. Maybe try one of these:

"Dad, there's a giraffe in your nose."

"Dad, I ate Mom's car for breakfast."

"Dad, I want to grow up to be a raccoon."

Good luck with your whisper experiment!

So, anyway. How did this all get started? Oh, right. Mutt whispered in reply to Stick Dog. Let's get back to it.

"What is it, Stick Dog?" Mutt whispered

back after taking his candy cane from his mouth. "What can we do for you?"

"Stay calm," Stick Dog whispered. "There are a bunch of humans gathering around this tree. There's nothing to worry about. I don't think any human is going to see us or come in here. I just think we need to be quiet. And don't take any more candy canes off the tree until they're gone. They might see one of our paws or something."

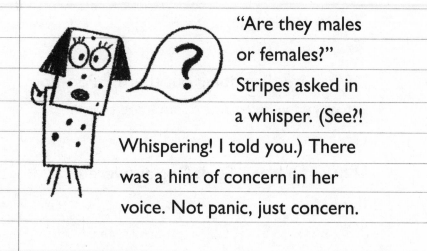

"Are they males or females?" Stripes asked in a whisper. (See?! Whispering! I told you.) There was a hint of concern in her voice. Not panic, just concern.

"Both," Stick Dog answered calmly.

"Are they big humans or little humans?" asked Karen.

"Both."

"Since we can't get any more candy canes right now, I'm just going to lick mine instead of bite it," Mutt commented. "That way it will last longer."

"Good thinking."

"What are they doing out there?" Poo-Poo asked.

"I have no idea," Stick Dog answered honestly.

But in three seconds, Stick Dog found out exactly what those humans were doing there.

And it was loud.

Chapter 7

STOP BEING SO BOSSY

All those humans—the males and the females, the big ones and the little ones— did the same thing at the same time.

Do you know what they did? I'll tell you.

They started singing.

For the first few seconds, it was quite startling to Stick Dog and his friends. After all, if it was sort of quiet one second and then a bunch of people started belting out a tune the next second, that would be kind of surprising, right? When those humans

started singing, Poo-Poo, Mutt, Karen, and
Stripes huddled a little bit closer to Stick Dog.

But just a little.

After those first few seconds, they settled
down, licked their candy canes, and listened
to the song—and commented quietly about
it among themselves.

"Why are these humans telling everybody
what to do?" Stripes asked between licks
of her candy cane. "I mean, we have to

watch out and not cry. And I don't even know what 'pout' means. They seem a little pushy, don't you think? Stop being so bossy. Jeez."

They listened a little longer.

"Okay, and who's Santa Claus?" asked Karen, tilting her head a bit. "And why's he coming to town all the time?"

They listened some more.

"I think this Santa human might be a spy," Poo-Poo suggested. "Sounds like kind of a sneaky character. It's like he's constantly

SANTA =

keeping an eye on everybody. I mean, could we get a little privacy?"

They licked their candy canes and continued to critique the music.

"Oh my gosh. He's coming back to town again," Karen said, shaking her head. "Just stick around, you know what I mean? All this back and forth. In and out of town. This Santa character is burning a lot of energy."

"I don't know about this human they're singing about," Mutt muttered. "But he sounds a little judgmental."

The song ended.

"I have a suggestion for this Santa Claus hooligan," Karen sighed. "Just move to town—and stay there. Life would be so much easier."

After the song ended, the humans gathered around the tree started to clap. Stick Dog  listened closely. He heard the humans talking among themselves for a minute or two and he heard the shuffling of shoes in the snow. It soon grew quiet outside of the tree. He was confident the humans had left.

"It's okay to get some more candy canes if you want," Stick Dog said to his friends, no longer whispering.

"Stick Dog?" Stripes said as she propped herself upright against the pine tree's trunk.

She needed to stretch higher because they had picked most of the candy canes on the lower branches.

"Yes?"

"What do you think that song was all about?" Stripes asked, snatching the candy cane she targeted. "What's the deal with this Santa guy?"

You could tell that Karen, Poo-Poo, and Mutt were curious too. They lifted their ears a bit and leaned toward Stick Dog to listen.

Now, Stick Dog had some sense of who Santa Claus was. He had seen pictures of him—in shops and house windows—at this time of year in the past. He wasn't quite certain, but he thought it had to do with a holiday—but he couldn't remember the name of it. He remembered and recognized decorations—twinkling lights, wreaths, and decorated trees like this one. He just didn't know the whole story. He could tell his friends didn't remember any of these things, just like they didn't remember that eating snow was a good way to quench their thirst in the winter.

"I'm not exactly sure," he answered honestly. "I think he has something to do with a holiday. I forget the name of it."

"I think this Santa fella is a suspicious character," said Poo-Poo. Karen, Mutt, and Stripes shared this sentiment. They nodded their heads. "I mean, watching everybody, keeping lists. He might be a bad dude."

"I doubt if he's bad," Stick Dog said. "I don't think those humans would sing a song about him if he was bad. It seemed like a nice song. It was a pretty tune and had a nice rhythm to it."

"It's a fair point," Stripes said.

"Stick Dog?"

"Yes, Karen?"

"My stomach doesn't feel very good," Karen said. Her tongue hung out of her mouth a bit

and her eyes were
a little droopy.

Stick Dog knew instantly what
had happened. They had each had three or
four of those delicious minty candy canes.
But Karen was much smaller than the rest of
their group. That many candy canes in a little
dachshund's stomach was way too much.

"I think you might have had too many candy
canes," Stick Dog said. "Does it sort of feel
like that?"

"Totally," she mumbled, scooting her
current half-eaten candy cane to the side.
"If I have any more, I'm going to explode."

"I don't want you to explode, Karen," Mutt
said softly and sincerely.

"Yeah, that would be bad," said Stripes.

"And what a mess," added Poo-Poo.

"Karen's not going to, umm, explode," Stick Dog said. "She'll be fine."

This assurance made everyone—even Karen—slightly more comfortable.

"You know what it feels like, Stick Dog?" she said.

"What?"

"It feels like we did things out of order," she answered. "It feels like we had dessert—way too much dessert—before we had dinner."

"So eating something that's not sweet might

help you feel better?" Stick Dog asked.

"I think so."

Stick Dog smiled. He knew just what to do.

Chapter 8

JERKY AND SANTA

"Let's go see Lucy," Stick Dog said.

This suggestion was met with great enthusiasm. Lucy, as you probably remember, is a German shepherd who lives in the back room of Mike's Magnificent Meats, a shop in town. They all met Lucy in the book *Stick Dog Meets His Match*.

LUCY

Since then, if the dogs have had a tough

time finding food, they will often visit Lucy. She can sneak them something from the meat shop.

There's something else you should probably know about Lucy. You know, just for background.

Stripes, Karen, Poo-Poo, and Mutt all suspect that Stick Dog and Lucy might have—how can I say this?—umm, romantic feelings.

Neither Stick Dog nor Lucy has ever admitted to this.

Okay, that's the background. Now, let's get back to the story.

"Mutt, before we leave can you carry some candy canes for us?" Stick Dog asked. "We might want some tomorrow."

"Absolutely," Mutt replied, always willing to help.

While Stripes, Karen, and Poo-Poo collected candy canes and pushed them into Mutt's fur, Stick Dog stuck his head out from under that big pine tree. There were no humans around at all. It would be a safe and quick trip to Mike's Magnificent Meats.

He scooted back under those low-hanging pine branches and turned to his friends.

"Let's go."

And they went.

They reached the alley behind Mike's Magnificent Meats in just a couple of minutes. Stick Dog went to the back door.

He tapped on it twice and then scratched it once. He and Lucy had created this code. She would know it was him.

Tap, tap, scraaaatch.

In nine seconds, Lucy opened the door. She could do it herself. She and her human, Mike, had hung a belt on the inside handle that Lucy could pull on to open the door. That way she could let herself out whenever she wanted.

"Hi, Stick Dog," Lucy said, and winked. She was clearly happy to see him.

"Hi. We thought you might be able to help us," he said, and smiled, stepping to the side so Lucy could see the others as well. "Karen had too many candy canes just now. We thought some more normal food might help her stomach."

"I had dessert before dinner," Karen explained. She already looked like she was feeling a bit better. "Crazy, right?!"

"Totally," Lucy said, smiling and opening the door wider. "Let's see what we can do. Come in, everybody."

"What about your human?" Stick Dog asked.

"He's asleep upstairs," Lucy explained. "It's been so busy at the store. It always is at this time of year. He went to bed early. We should try to be quiet, but he never wakes up."

"Okay. Great," Stick Dog said.

"Stay here and I'll see what I can find in the store," Lucy said, and then left that back room.

"It smells so good in here," Poo-Poo said quietly. His nose was in the air.

Mutt, Karen, and Stripes were all taking in the aromas too. They had settled in near a big silver refrigerator and a long table. The table had a stained white apron, two big knives, and three thick rolls of shiny aluminum foil on it.

"It's . . . it's . . . it's . . . ," Stripes said, trying to think of the right word.

Mutt came up with it.

He said, "It's meat-a-licious!"

Lucy came back with a plastic container in her mouth. She set it down on the floor and pulled the lid off with her mouth.

"This is beef jerky," she announced. "It's dry and chewy. And really tasty. We have bunches of these containers. I don't think Mike will notice if one is missing."

All six dogs positioned themselves in a circle around that container and took pieces of jerky out. Stick Dog and Lucy sat close together. There were dozens of pieces inside so there was plenty for everybody. The beef jerky was delicious, salty and chewy. It took a while to eat it, so there was plenty of time to talk.

Stick Dog told Lucy about hiding inside the big pine tree and discovering the candy canes. Mutt shook a couple of candy canes from his fur and gave them to Lucy. And they told her about the humans gathering around the pine tree and singing.

"Lots of humans sing Christmas songs at this time of year," Lucy said. "They're called Christmas carols."

"*Christmas*," Stick Dog said. "I was trying to remember that name. We don't know much about it."

"You don't?" Lucy asked. She seemed pretty surprised.

"Not really," Stick Dog answered, reaching for another piece of beef jerky. He held it out to Lucy first, but she shook her head politely at his offer. "You know, we're strays. It seems like it's more of a human holiday."

"Of course. That makes perfectly good sense," Lucy said and nodded. "I know a lot about it. I hear humans talk about it all the time here in the store—especially little humans. They get really excited about it. And since I have Mike, I've experienced some Christmas things myself."

"Can you tell us about Christmas?" Stick Dog asked.

"I'd be happy to," Lucy answered. "What do you want to know?"

They had plenty of questions for Lucy.

"First of all, who is this Santa Claus that everybody is singing about?" Poo-Poo asked. "He sounds a little suspicious to me—slightly sneaky."

"And he just keeps coming to town and coming to town and coming to town," Karen moaned. "I mean, get there already! You know what I mean?"

"Does Santa Claws actually have, you know, real claws?" Stripes asked. She seemed a little frightened. "Like sharp, dangerous claws? Is that how he got his name?"

"Santa definitely does not have sharp claws," Lucy began. "He is a nice, male human who lives at the North Pole."

"I've never heard of that place before," Poo-Poo said, and shrugged. "Where is it? What direction?"

"It's, umm, north," Lucy said kind of slowly. "North is the direction."

"Hunh," Poo-Poo said, shrugging again. "Go figure."

"He has a big factory there where elves live and make toys and gifts," Lucy continued. "And he really only comes to town once a year. It's tomorrow night, as a matter of fact. Tomorrow is Christmas Eve—the day before Christmas."

"What are elves?" Stripes asked.

"I'm not totally sure to be honest," Lucy

answered. "I think they are very small humans who are really good at making presents."

"That's kind of like me," Karen said.

Stick Dog asked, "How so?"

"I'm a very small dog who is really good at chasing her tail."

"Oh, umm, sure," Lucy said, glancing sideways at Stick Dog for a second. "Yes, that's a very good comparison."

Then Karen chased her tail.

Lucy had much more information

about Christmas to share with them.

Some things sounded fun.

Some sounded strange.

And some sounded outrageous.

Chapter 9

WOW

"What does this sneaky Santa character look like anyway?" Poo-Poo asked. "Is he dressed in black, like a ninja? Or maybe he just wears underwear like a professional wrestler?"

"Not exactly."

Mutt placed his beef jerky to the side. He was interested in all of this too. "Does he have a long neck like a giraffe?"

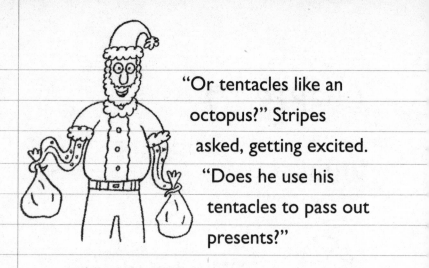

"Or tentacles like an octopus?" Stripes asked, getting excited. "Does he use his tentacles to pass out presents?"

"No. Humans generally don't have long giraffe necks or, umm, octopus tentacles," Lucy said quietly. "He's kind of a big, older human. He has a fluffy white beard. And he wears a bright red suit."

"You can't be sneaky in a bright red suit!" Poo-Poo exclaimed.

"Shh," Stick Dog whispered, and pointed up, reminding his friends that Lucy's roommate, Mike, was sleeping upstairs.

"He's not sneaky," Lucy said. "I'm sorry I'm not explaining things very well. Santa Claus is good. Exceptionally good. He comes late at night on Christmas Eve to give presents to everybody—mostly small humans."

"Why does he come to this particular town?" asked Stick Dog.

"Oh, he goes to every town," Lucy replied. "Not just this town."

"Every town around here?" Stick Dog asked.

"Every town in the whole world," Lucy said.

Stick Dog opened his eyes wide. This seemed hard to believe, but Lucy nodded her head at him and said, "It's true."

"He must be pretty tired by the end of the night," Karen said as she stopped chasing her tail. "I mean, think of all the towns in the world. There must be a lot. Seven or eight—maybe more."

"How does he have time to go to all those towns?" Stripes asked.

"I think it's kind of magical," Lucy replied. "Everybody knows he can do it. He does it every year."

"Wow," Poo-Poo said, expressing the whole group's attitude. "That's impressive."

"You know what's really impressive, Lucy?" Karen asked.

Lucy grinned and asked, "What?"

"The way I can chase my tail! Watch!"

Then Karen started chasing her tail some more.

"I think she's feeling better," Lucy whispered, leaning close to Stick Dog.

"I think so too," Stick Dog said, watching Karen. He was certainly happy about Karen's improved condition, but his expression showed a little confusion too. He turned back to Lucy. "Some of this Santa Claus stuff sounds kind of peculiar. What else can you tell us about Christmas?"

"Santa leaves presents under the Christmas tree," Lucy continued, explaining the additional things she knew about Christmas. "Or in stockings."

Mutt asked, "What are stockings?"

"They're kind of like big socks," Lucy said. "You hang them by a fireplace or from a shelf. Then Santa comes in and puts a gift inside the stocking."

"What's this Christmas tree thingamajig?" Stripes asked.

"Humans bring pine trees inside their houses and decorate them," Lucy said. "The tree with the candy canes that you told me about was a Christmas tree."

"That was outside," Poo-Poo said.

"They can be outside too," Lucy explained. "But mostly inside."

"Humans do strange things," Mutt said. "I mean, trees are supposed to be outside, not inside."

Lucy smiled and said, "It's just a tradition, I think."

"Hold on a second," Karen said. She stopped chasing her tail again. You could tell something was bothering her. "How does Santa get into everybody's house?"

"He comes down the chimney," Lucy said matter-of-factly.

"What?!" Poo-Poo and Stripes yelped at the same time.

"Shh," Stick Dog reminded them, pointing up at the ceiling again.

"Down the chimney," Lucy repeated. Stick Dog watched her and listened intently. A lot of what she had said sounded very strange—bizarre even. If he didn't know Lucy so well, he would probably think she was making all of this up. But he did  know her well—and trusted her. There was also something about the way she was describing all these fascinating Christmas details. She wasn't exaggerating anything. She just seemed to be stating the facts. He believed Lucy.

"Let me get this straight," Poo-Poo said, shaking his head a bit. He, unlike Stick Dog, obviously had a great many doubts. "Santa wears a bright red suit, travels all over the world in one night, goes down a bunch of chimneys, and leaves presents in big socks and under trees that are inside? Is that what you're saying?!"

Lucy nodded.

"I just don't see how he has time to do all that," Mutt said.

"He has help," Lucy said.

"Who helps him?" Karen asked.

"Eight reindeer."

"What's a reindeer?" Poo-Poo asked. "Is it like the deer we see in the woods?"

"I think they might be similar or related," Lucy answered. "But there are certainly differences."

"Indeed. Yes. There can be different types of the same animal," Poo-Poo (a poodle) confirmed. He liked showing off his smartness. He looked at Lucy (a German shepherd), then Stripes (a Dalmatian), and Karen (a dachshund), and added, "I can't think of an animal with different types right now, but I believe it's true."

"Well, Santa's reindeer are quite large," Lucy continued. "They're very strong and have big antlers. And they can do something quite unusual—quite magical."

"What can they do?" asked Stick Dog.

"You're not going to believe it."

Chapter 10

WHAT ABOUT US?

"Santa's reindeer can fly," Lucy said.

"Fly?!" Stripes yelped.

"Shh," Stick Dog said again, pointing up.

Karen, Poo-Poo, and Mutt stared wide-eyed at Lucy. They couldn't believe what they had just heard.

"That's right," Lucy said. "They can fly. They pull Santa's giant sleigh from town to town. The sleigh is packed with the things the elves have made at the North Pole—toys and presents."

"Then he takes the presents down the chimney and puts them in the stockings and under the Christmas tree," Stripes said, shaking her head in wonder. "This Santa guy is one awesome dude!"

"I want to get in on some of this Christmas action," Karen said with a twinkle in her eye.

"Has Santa left you presents at Christmas, Lucy?" Stick Dog asked.

"Every year," Lucy said, and nodded. "My human, Mike, hangs my stocking over the fireplace. And he puts

up a Christmas tree that's covered with
decorations and lights. The lights can be
different colors or just white. We use little
white ones."

"And?" Stripes asked.

"And on Christmas morning, there's a
present in my stocking—and a present
under the tree," Lucy said. "And the
cookies are all gone. Santa has eaten them
all—or taken them along to snack on during
his journey."

"Cookies?" Mutt asked. "What cookies?"

"Oh, didn't I mention that?" Lucy replied.
"It's a tradition to leave cookies for Santa.
Mike and I always leave cookies. It's such a
busy night for Santa, you want to keep him

well fed—and it's a way to say thank you. Everybody in the world leaves him cookies."

"That must be millions of cookies," Stick Dog said.

"I doubt if he eats them all," Lucy said. "He probably feeds some to his reindeer. Maybe he takes a lot back to the North Pole to give to the elves. I'm not sure though."

"All of this is amazing," Stripes whispered, still shaking her head a bit. "What kind of presents do you get, Lucy?"

"Oh, there's usually a big rawhide bone. Or a squeaky toy. I got a nice yellow rope last year."

All of this was such incredible news with so many interesting—and almost unimaginable—details that the dogs sat there in silence. They thought about everything Lucy had said about Christmas. They visualized flying reindeer and stockings stuffed with gifts.

"I'm not sure I can believe it," Poo-Poo said after thirty seconds or so. "It's just too much. Too many strange things."

"Wait just a second," Karen said to Lucy. Something entirely different was bothering her. "How come Santa brings *you* presents every year, but not *me*? I've been good. I'm never naughty. Except sometimes when I drink coffee, I go a little crazy—but those are the only times. You don't happen to have any coffee around here, do you? I love coffee!"

"No, I don't have any coffee," Lucy answered kindly and honestly.

"What about shoes, Lucy?" asked Mutt with a sense of urgency in his voice. "Do you have any of those?"

"I'm sorry, no," Lucy said. "But I know to keep an eye out for shoes for you, Mutt. I won't forget."

Mutt smiled and nodded.

Stripes sat back on her rear haunches and brought a paw up to her chin. "It's interesting though—what Karen said. Why doesn't he leave presents for us? What about us?"

"Yeah," Poo-Poo said. "What about us?"

"I've been thinking about that," Lucy said.
"And I think I might know why."

"Why?" asked Stick Dog. He was curious too.

"I suspect that he doesn't know about
Stick Dog's pipe," Lucy said. "I don't think
he knows where you live. He's used to
visiting houses and apartment buildings
and places where humans live—and where
lots of dogs and other animals live too.
I think he probably flies right over Stick
Dog's pipe—and has no idea that you all

stay there with him."

"So, if we could just let Santa know where Stick Dog's pipe is," said Karen slowly.

"And get some stockings," added Stripes.

"And decorate a pine tree," said Mutt.

"And leave him some cookies," Poo-Poo pitched in.

"Then maybe," concluded Stick Dog, "just maybe Santa would visit my pipe and leave us

Christmas presents."

"It's possible," Lucy said. "But there's one big problem."

"What's that?" asked Stick Dog.

"Tomorrow is Christmas Eve," Lucy answered. "You have to do all that stuff before Santa comes tomorrow night."

"That's a lot of work," Stick Dog said quietly.

"I tell you what," Lucy said. "I'll sneak some extra cookies and you can come get them tomorrow night. That's one less thing you have to worry about. And you can take the rest of this beef jerky right now. That way you won't have to spend time looking for food tomorrow."

"Thanks." Stick Dog nodded and smiled, already feeling a little better. "We better go. Lots to do—and not much time to do it."

Chapter 11

GIANTS

When the five dogs got back to Stick Dog's pipe that night, they fell asleep quickly. They were tired from the trip back and forth to town. Their bellies were full of beef jerky and candy canes. And they huddled together comfortably for warmth. They slept deeply—and for a long time.

So when they woke in the early afternoon on Christmas Eve, they were clear-eyed and well rested.

"It's Christmas Eve," Stick Dog reminded his friends from the entrance to his pipe.

The sun was out. The snow-covered meadow in front of his pipe—and the snow-covered trees around the meadow—sparkled in the sun. "We have lots to do if we want Santa Claus to come here tonight. We need to find stockings, get a Christmas tree, and figure out a way to let Santa Claus know we live in this pipe."

Stripes sighed and said, "That's an awful lot to do."

"As long as we work together, we can do anything," Stick Dog said with absolute conviction. "We'll do one thing at a time. Let's start with the stockings. How can we get or make five of those?"

"What are stockings again?" Stripes asked.

"Really big socks," Stick Dog answered.

"This is going to be easier than I thought," Poo-Poo said casually. "I already got the whole stocking thing figured out."

"You do?" Stick Dog asked.

"Sure. Easy stuff," Poo-Poo answered. He leaned back against the wall of the pipe, shifting his shoulders back and forth a little bit to get comfortable.

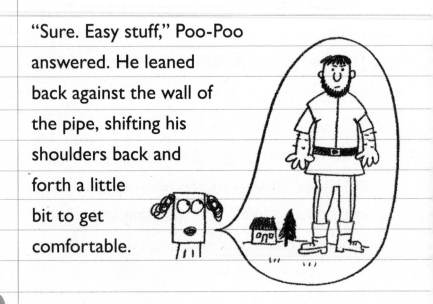

"We just need to find some giants."

"Giants?" Stick Dog asked.

"Giants," Poo-Poo confirmed. "Giants have huge feet. We just need to find some giants and sneak into where they live. We wait for them to fall asleep and then pull their great big socks off their great big feet."

"How many giants do we need to find, Poo-Poo?" asked Mutt as he picked through his pile of shoes. He chose an old leather work boot to chew on.

"Let's see," Poo-Poo said, doing the math. "We need five stockings. Giants have two feet each. So we need to find two and a half giants to get five socks. Finding half a giant might be a tad difficult, but we'll figure it out."

"Umm," Stick Dog said slowly. He couldn't decide if he wanted to talk about the math part of Poo-Poo's plan or the whole plan itself. This slight hesitation allowed Karen to help with the math.

"I think finding half a giant might be hard too," she said. "How about if we find one two-legged giant and one three-legged giant?"

"Works for me," Poo-Poo said. "Whatever."

"Or we could find five one-legged giants," Stripes suggested.

$\times 5$

"That's okay too."

Mutt seemed to agree with all this, nodding slightly as he chewed on the boot.

"It's settled then," Poo-Poo said. He gave his body a quick shiver and shake, preparing to leave. Karen and Stripes took a couple of steps toward the pipe's opening. Mutt stopped chewing on the boot, dropped it, and stood up.

"Poo-Poo, can I ask you something about giants before we leave?" Stick Dog asked. "I just want to make sure I know what I'm looking for—and you seem to know a lot about the subject."

"Of course," he answered. "But let's make it quick. We are about to go giant hunting, you know."

"Okay, I will," Stick Dog replied, picking up the pace of his words a bit. "Giants are really big humans, right?"

"Right. They're gigantic."

"Really tall?"

"Super-extra tall."

"Twice as tall as a regular human?"

"No, no, Stick Dog. You're not understanding giants at all," Poo-Poo said with an understanding tone of voice. It sounded like he often had to explain the most obvious things to Stick Dog. "Giants are

enormous. They're taller than trees. Way taller than trees. Their heads get lost in the clouds sometimes."

"So you can see them from miles and miles away then?"

"Most definitely," Poo-Poo acknowledged as he moved toward the pipe's opening. "Come on, everybody!"

"Where are you all going?" Stick Dog asked as Poo-Poo, Mutt, Stripes, and Karen were about to exit his pipe.

"On the giant hunt," Stripes said.

"But you don't have to go anywhere," Stick Dog declared. "You can just look out from my pipe. Just look above the trees and if you see any giants, we'll run toward where they are."

"Hunh?" Poo-Poo asked, turning his head over his shoulder to look at Stick Dog.

"You don't have to go anywhere," Stick Dog repeated. "That's the true genius of your plan, Poo-Poo. I really admire you for it."

"Wait. Umm. What exactly is the genius of my plan?"

"Looking for giants," Stick Dog explained. "They're so big that you can see them from miles and miles away. You said so yourself. Way taller than trees. Get their heads lost in the clouds. We don't have to go anywhere. Just look out my pipe and if you see any giants, we'll run in that direction straightaway. That is what's so smart about your plan. We don't even have to go anywhere searching for giants. They're so big, we'll be able to see them from here."

"Wow," Poo-Poo said quietly. He pointed at his head. "I really *am* a genius."

"You sure are," Stick Dog said.

And with that, Mutt, Stripes, Karen, and Poo-Poo went and stood at the entrance of the pipe. Stick Dog did too. They peered over the treetops. They looked up toward the clouds. They searched in every direction.

No giants.

"That's disappointing," Poo-Poo said.

"It's not disappointing at all," Stick Dog
said. "That's another reason your plan is so
good—it's extraordinary really."

"Why's that?"

"Giants are so, so, so big," Stick Dog said,
"that we'll see them immediately as soon
as they show up in the area. Once we see
some giants, we'll execute your plan."

This made Poo-Poo feel better.

"Until then," Stick Dog said as he waved

his friends back into the pipe where it
was warmer, "let's work on a backup plan.
Where else can we find stockings? Or what
else could we use instead of stockings?"

Stripes had an idea.

Chapter 12

FISH

"We can use fish for stockings," Stripes said.

"Excuse me?" Stick Dog said. "Did you say fish?"

"That's right," she affirmed. "Fish."

They all came farther back into the pipe.

Poo-Poo and Karen settled on the old couch cushion. Mutt returned to chew on the boot. And Stripes paced back and forth among them all as she explained her idea.

"How do we use fish?" Stick Dog asked. "They don't have feet. They don't wear socks."

"I know that, silly," Stripes said. "We don't use fish socks. We use the fish themselves."

"I'm not sure what you mean," Stick Dog said honestly. He wanted to keep this moving. They had slept later than usual— and they had a lot to do. "Maybe you could provide some details."

"No problem," Stripes said. "The thing is we don't need stockings exactly. We just need to hang up something that Santa can put presents in. And I think fish would do the trick."

"Umm. How so?"

"We just go down to the creek," Stripes continued. "We catch five fish. You know, wait for them to swim by and snatch them. Then we bring the fish back, hang them up with their mouths open, and then Santa puts presents inside the fish. Tomorrow morning we wake up and pull the presents out of the fish. Then we'll take  the fish back to the creek and let them swim away. Easy-peasy, mac-and-cheesy."

Stick Dog struggled to come up with something to say. He knew Stripes's fish plan had all kinds of problems. Breaking through the icy creek. Catching five fish with their bare paws. Figuring out how to hang them up. And, of course, the fish would not live out of water. They couldn't just take them back to the creek on Christmas morning. Then he thought of something.

"I really like your plan, Stripes," Stick Dog said. "It's clever and innovative. I doubt if anyone has ever thought of using fish as Christmas stockings before."

"I am quite clever, it's true."

"There's just one tiny thing I'm worried about."

"What's that?"

"What if the fish eat our presents?!" Stick Dog asked. "We'll wake up and the fish will be empty. No presents at all. It will be very disappointing."

"Do you think they'd really eat our presents?" Karen asked.

"Without a doubt," Stick Dog replied. "Fish will eat anything. They eat worms. And flies and bugs on top of the water. Eating a Christmas present will be like a gourmet meal for a fish that's used to eating worms and bugs."

"Shoot," Stripes said, disappointed. Her tail drooped. "I think you might be right. They might actually eat our presents. My plan won't work."

"Hey, Stripes," Stick Dog said quickly, sensing her disappointment. "That's not your fault—it's the fault of those gosh-darned, present-eating fish. They're the ones who messed up your excellent plan."

"Erggh," Stripes growled, changing and redirecting her emotions. "I've never liked fish. They're so slippery."

Stick Dog was happy to have the use-fish-for-Christmas-stockings plan behind him. He figured Karen and Mutt would offer ideas too. He turned to Karen first.

"What about you, Karen?" he asked. "Do you have any ideas?"

"I do have an idea," Karen said happily as she sprang up from the old couch cushion. "I do indeed."

"Great. What is it?"

"I think I should chase my tail now!"

"No, I mean about the—" Stick Dog said, and then stopped himself as Karen began to chase her tail. He smiled at her and walked over to Mutt, who was chewing slowly and rhythmically on that boot.

Mutt noticed Stick Dog, dropped the boot, and said, "I've been thinking about something. Chewing on shoes really helps me think. Gives me time to ponder things. You know, reflect."

"What have you been thinking about?" Stick Dog asked.

"The way humans use shoes," Mutt said. "It doesn't make sense to me."

"Why not?"

"Why would humans want to put their feet in shoes when they could chew on shoes

MM-MMM.

instead? I mean, chewing is way better than wearing. Why would you waste a perfectly chewable shoe just to put something inside it? That's messed up."

Stick Dog stopped. He didn't stop because he needed to explain to Mutt that humans don't typically, you know, chew on shoes. He stopped for another reason. He held stone-still. He didn't move a muscle. There was something Mutt just said.

Then his head twitched. It tilted. Stick Dog had it.

"I know what we can use for stockings," he whispered.

Chapter 13

KAREN IS SPARKLY

"What are we going to use for stockings, Stick Dog?" Poo-Poo asked.

"Mutt's collection of shoes," Stick Dog answered. "I think his shoes will work."

"I think you're confusing what humans wear on their strange feet," Stripes said, coming closer. All of them gathered around Stick

Dog now. Karen even stopped chasing her tail to join in. "Christmas stockings are like socks. They're not like shoes."

"I understand the difference between socks and shoes," Stick Dog said. "But if we hang up the shoes with their openings at the top, maybe Santa Claus will understand we're just substituting the shoes for stockings."

"I think Stick Dog might actually be right about that," Poo-Poo agreed. "Stockings, socks, shoes, whatever. They're kind of all the same thing anyway. They cover human feet. Plus, this Santa fella seems like a pretty bright guy. I think he'll make the connection."

Poo-Poo's endorsement had a positive effect on Stripes, Mutt, and Karen. After listening to Poo-Poo, the others all agreed to Stick Dog's shoe plan.

"Mutt?" Stick Dog asked. "Would it be okay if we use five of your shoes as Christmas stockings?"

"Of course," Mutt answered immediately. "No problem."

And with that, they all went to Mutt's pile of shoes. They pawed through them, pushing and scooching the shoes all around the floor of Stick Dog's pipe. They held up individual shoes and examined them closely.

The choosing went pretty quickly.

Mutt decided on the work boot he'd chewed on earlier.

There was a large
pair of black-and-
white basketball
sneakers. Poo-Poo
picked the right
one and Stripes picked the left one.

"I really like this purple one that has
shiny glitter on the material," Karen said,
examining the shoe closely. "It's a little
small, but it suits my personality!"

"How so?" Mutt asked.

"It sparkles!" Karen said. "And I'm sparkly!"

Stick Dog picked an orange-and-black
running shoe to use as his stocking.

"Now what do we do?" Poo-Poo asked.

"We need to hang them up," Stick Dog said, looking around. "Lucy said humans often hang their stockings up near fireplaces. We don't have one of those. And I'm not sure there's anywhere in here that we could hang them. Santa might not even come in here. We don't exactly have a chimney. But there has to be somewhere to put them."

They looked all around—left and right, up and down—for a place to hang those shoes. But they had no luck at all. Stick Dog realized the main problem quickly. The walls of his pipe were curved, of course. It would be practically impossible to hang anything on them.

Then he looked outside.

"I got it," he said, and smiled. "I know what

we can do."

"What?" Karen asked.

"We'll hang them at the opening of my pipe. We can hang them over the top edge. There's some room up there because the pipe juts out of the hillside."

Poo-Poo, Mutt, Karen, and Stripes all tilted their heads as they looked at Stick Dog with confused expressions.

"Hunh?" Poo-Poo asked, speaking for the four of them.

"Come on," Stick Dog said, and nodded his head toward the pipe's entrance. "I'll show you what I mean. Bring your shoes."

Stick Dog's pipe ran through a huge hill. On top of the hill was Highway 16. The pipe was very big and round. It had to be for five dogs to live in, after all. The pipe extended from the hill a few feet out into the meadow. Because it did, some of the pipe's top was exposed. And that's where Stick Dog led his friends.

They had been up to that part of the hillside above the pipe plenty of times. It was a nice place to lounge around on a nice day. Sometimes, Stick Dog would go up there to enjoy the view—and he liked being able to stretch his neck down and look into the pipe to see how his friends were doing.

"So, just exactly how is this going to work?" Poo-Poo asked.

Again, Stick Dog decided to show his friends. He talked as he did. He dropped his orange-and-black shoe and got started.

"First, we each need to find a pretty big rock," Stick Dog said, and began to paw and scratch at the snow. It wasn't difficult—the snow was only five inches deep and it was the fluffy kind, not the icy kind. He also

knew there were tons
of rocks up here. He
found one in fourteen
seconds and held it up
for his friends to see. "About this size."

Mutt, Karen, Stripes, and Poo-Poo all did
exactly what Stick Dog had just done. They
dropped their shoes, pawed and scratched
at the snow, and found four other similarly
sized rocks. Stick Dog had to help Karen
dig hers out—it was kind of frozen in the
ground.

"Pull the shoestrings up to the top of the
shoe," Stick Dog said, demonstrating again
as he spoke. "Now hang the shoe down
over the pipe with the open part at the top.
Twist the end of the shoestrings into a ball
and put the rock down on the balled-up

shoestrings like this."

They watched Stick Dog. They leaned
their heads over the top of the pipe.
Stick Dog's shoe was hanging there—and
swinging gently.

"No way," Karen said. "It totally worked!"

They all used Stick Dog's method to hang
their own shoes over the entrance to his
pipe. It didn't work for everybody the first
time. Two times the shoestrings slid out
from under the rocks and they had to go

down, pick up the shoe, and try again. And Mutt hung his shoe upside down the first time.

But with Stick Dog's help, all five shoes were hanging securely in less than ten minutes.

They hurried back into the pipe to warm up.

Stick Dog looked up at the sun. These winter days were short. It was late afternoon now— and they still had a lot to do.

Chapter 14

LONG-TERM PLANNING

The five dogs admired their hanging shoe-stockings from inside Stick Dog's pipe. They gnawed and chewed on pieces of beef jerky as they did.

"Okay, the stockings are up and they look great," Stripes said, and chewed. "What do we need to do next, Stick Dog?"

"Three more things," he answered quickly. "We have to get and decorate a Christmas tree. Then I have to go to Lucy's and get some cookies to leave for Santa tonight. And we still have to figure out a way to let him know that we live here."

"How are we going to do that?" asked Karen.

"I have no idea," he answered honestly. "But let's work on the Christmas tree first. There are plenty of pine trees in the forest. We just need to cut one down and bring it back here."

"How are we going to cut down a pine tree?" asked Poo-Poo.

"I know how to do it," said Karen quickly. "All we need is an ax. A great big ax. That's what you need to cut down a tree. Do you have a great big ax, Stick Dog?"

"Umm, no."

"Mutt," Karen called over. Mutt was at the shoe pile, trying to pick out a new one to chew on—because the work boot was now hanging at the entrance to Stick Dog's pipe. "Do you have a great big ax in your fur?"

"I don't think so, but let me check."

With that, Mutt splayed his legs out and gave his whole body a tremendous five-second

shake. Lots of things came out, including a yellow mitten, two bottle caps, three broken pencils, and one candy cane.

But no ax.

"I don't seem to have an ax," Mutt said, looking around at the stuff scattered about him on the floor of the pipe.

"No problem. I have another idea anyway," Karen replied, and turned back to Stick Dog.

"Do you have a chain saw?" she asked him. "I'm pretty sure you can use a chain saw to cut down trees."

"No. I, umm, don't have a chain saw."

Karen jerked her head toward Mutt again

and asked, "How about a chain saw? Do you have a chain saw in your fur?"

"It's possible, I guess," Mutt replied. "Let's see."

Mutt shook again—this time for seven seconds. Several more things flew out, including a paper cup, a pink eraser, a napkin, and three more bottle caps.

But no chain saw.

"No chain saw," Mutt declared, and shook his head.

"Are you sure you don't have a great big ax or a chain saw, Stick Dog?" Karen asked—turning back to him a final time.

"Positive."

"Well, jeez, Stick Dog," Stripes said. "Then what do you do when you want to cut down a tree?"

"I've never wanted to cut down a tree before."

"You haven't?" asked Poo-Poo.

"No."

"What about at Christmastime?" Karen asked. "When Santa comes and all that jazz?"

"We just learned about Christmastime and Santa and, umm, all that jazz from Lucy last night," Stick Dog explained slowly. He was starting to feel a little pressure near his forehead, behind his eyes—like he might be getting a headache.

"And you didn't get an ax or a chain saw between then and now?" Mutt asked. He had decided to chew on a fancy silver high-heeled shoe.

"You mean between late last night and right now?"

"That's right," Poo-Poo said.

 "Umm, no," Stick Dog answered quietly. He closed his eyes and rubbed his paws

against his temples. "I didn't."

"You should really learn to plan better, Stick Dog," Karen said. "Look ahead. Have a real strategy. You know what I mean?"

"I'll, umm, work on that, I guess," Stick Dog said. The rubbing helped relieve that pressure a bit. He wanted to get back to the topic at hand. "Let's all think about how we could possibly cut—"

"Stick Dog," Karen interrupted.

"Yes?"

"Would you like me to demonstrate what good, long-term planning looks like?"

"Sure. Go ahead."

"Okay, watch."

"I'm watching."

"I plan to chase my tail."

Then Karen chased her tail. She chased it for twenty-three seconds and stopped.

"See," she panted after stopping. "I planned ahead. Really thought about chasing my tail

strategically. And then I put my plan into action. I like to be proactive. I think you could have done the same thing with an ax and a chain saw."

"I see. Thanks for the advice," Stick Dog said. He was ready—really, really ready—to move on. "I tell you what, let's head out into the woods and choose a pine tree and then see if anything comes to mind."

Since Stick Dog had not planned ahead and gathered an ax or a chain saw since late last night—and since their bellies were full of beef jerky—Karen, Poo-Poo, Mutt, and Stripes decided to go with him into the forest.

Because there were dozens of pine trees nearby—they could, in fact, see several from Stick Dog's pipe as they exited—finding a pine tree was not a problem.

Choosing the best one took some time.

They ruled out a couple of tiny saplings. And dismissed three massive pine trees that were clumped together in a group. After discussing the merits of several others, they settled on a medium-sized tree that was about five feet tall. It was at the edge of the meadow. Not very far from Stick Dog's pipe at all.

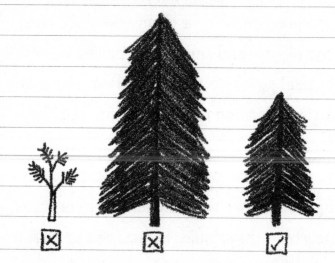

"Where are we going to put this tree after we cut it down?" Stripes asked.

"I thought maybe right outside my pipe,"

Stick Dog answered quickly. He had already been thinking about this subject. "If we put it there, it might be a good clue for Santa. It might make him think that somebody lives inside the pipe."

"Who lives inside the pipe, Stick Dog?" Karen asked.

"Umm, we do."

"Right, right."

"The question is," Stick Dog said, "how are we going to get this tree from here to my pipe?"

"I could bash into it with my head," Poo-Poo said without hesitation. He began to back away from the tree to gain enough room to charge and gain speed. "That seems like the most obvious way to do it. A few good head cracks by yours truly just might do the trick."

"No, Poo-Poo," Stick Dog said with just a hint of firmness in his voice. He definitely didn't want him bashing into the pine tree's thick, hard trunk. "You are, without question, the best head-basher I've ever known. But even you can't knock a big tree down. It's not like a garbage can or something. It's got strong, deep roots."

"Well, I'm ready if you change your mind," Poo-Poo said, walking back. "There's nothing like some good head-bashing. Just say the word."

"Umm, okay," Stick Dog replied, and began to circle the tree slowly. "Will do."

Mutt, Karen, Poo-Poo, and Stripes watched him.

"It would take something hard and sharp to cut that trunk," he said quietly as he circled. He was thinking out loud more than talking to his friends. "There's nothing  sharp and hard in the forest. And there's nothing sharp and hard back in my pipe."

"Our teeth are sharp and hard," Stripes suggested.

"That's certainly true," Stick Dog said, still pacing. "But it would take us days and days to chew through a tree trunk. And it would probably hurt our teeth."

"I think we're looking at this the wrong way," Stripes said.

"How so?" asked Poo-Poo.

"We're trying to take the tree back all at once," Stripes said. "That's too big a problem to solve."

"What do you suggest we do?" asked Mutt.

"We take it back in pieces," Stripes said.

"Take it back a branch at a time and then put it together outside Stick Dog's pipe. We may not be able to chew through the trunk, but we can certainly chew through some of these branches."

"How do we put it back together?" asked Karen.

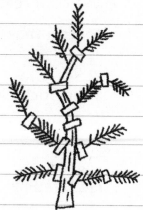

"Oh, just with glue or some tape or whatever," Stripes said simply. "Mutt's probably got something in his fur that we can use."

"But we still need the trunk to put it back together," Poo-Poo said. "And we already know we can't chew through that in time."

"Shoot," Stripes said, and shook her head

back and forth three times. "You're right.
Dang it!"

Stick Dog had continued to circle that tree
while his friends discussed Stripes's plan.
He had dismissed it as soon as he heard
it. They couldn't bite the tree to pieces
and then reassemble all the pieces. And, of
course, they would need the trunk to do it.

Then Stick Dog stopped
circling the tree.

He tilted his head.

He raised an eyebrow.

There was an idea there. He just had to find
it. What was it?

Then he found it. He looked at his friends
and smiled.

"We don't need the trunk," he said. "I know
what we can do."

Chapter 15

KAREN HOPS ON

"What can we do, Stick Dog?" Mutt asked.

"Stripes helped me figure it out," Stick Dog said, coming closer. "But we do need some branches. And, like Stripes said, I think we can chew through some of these lower branches for sure."

"Then what do we do with them?" Poo-Poo asked.

Stick Dog looked up at the sky. They had woken up late. And figuring out how to use shoes for stockings and choosing this particular pine tree had all taken a great deal of time. The sun was already sinking toward the horizon.

"If it's okay with you guys, I'd like to tell you when we get some branches back to my pipe," Stick Dog said. He felt anxious about the time they had left in the day. He still had to get to Lucy's, get some cookies, and figure out how to let Santa know where his pipe was. "It's getting late."

"I don't know, Stick Dog," Stripes said with doubt in her voice. "We trusted you to have an ax or a chain saw and that didn't work out very well, did it?"

"Umm, no. No, it didn't," Stick Dog replied. "But this time you can trust me for sure. I promise. I've got a plan. I just can't tell you about it while I'm chewing through some of these branches."

This was enough for Mutt, Karen, Stripes, and Poo-Poo to agree.

And with that, they all began biting, gnawing, chewing, and munching through some of that pine tree's branches. They bit thin ones. They gnawed thick ones. They chewed short ones. They munched long ones.

It was tough work—and it took a long time. But they kept at it with energy and enthusiasm. They hoped, after all, that their hard work would pay off that night with a visit from Santa Claus.

"Okay, that should do it," Stick Dog said, placing another branch on their small pile. He inhaled and exhaled deeply three times. "Let's drag these back to my pipe and I'll show you what I have in mind."

It was not a very long trip back to the pipe.

Mutt, Poo-Poo, Stripes, and Stick Dog grabbed two or three branches in their mouths and began to drag them backward through the snow. It wasn't difficult for them.

It was difficult, however, for Karen. She wanted to carry just as many as her friends. She wanted to do her part.

But she was shorter. Her legs didn't move through the snow with as much power and speed as the others. When Poo-Poo, Mutt, Stripes, and Stick Dog got to the pipe in a couple of minutes, Karen was still struggling at the far edge of the meadow.

Stick Dog hustled out to her.

"Hi, Karen," he said upon arrival. "Can I ask you to do me a favor?"

"Sure," Karen panted after dropping the branches from her mouth. You could tell that she was grateful to take a break. "What can I do for you, Stick Dog?"

"Well, it's about these branches you're dragging across the meadow."

"What about them?"

"They just happen to be the exact branches that I chewed off that tree personally," Stick Dog replied. He didn't know this, of course. All the branches pretty much looked the same. But he didn't divulge this to Karen. "And they're special to me. I sort of created a special bond with them."

"A special bond?"

"That's right," Stick Dog said, and nodded. "A special branch-to-dog bond. And because of that bond—that unique and superior relationship—I thought maybe you might let me bring the branches the rest of the way back to my pipe."

Karen inhaled deeply and tried to hide her relief. She said, "Well, it's not like I was struggling with them or anything. I'm just as strong and powerful as you guys."

"Oh, I know," Stick Dog said. "I've seen

you chase your tail. I see your power when you do that."

"Yes, yes. It's quite obvious when I do a bit of tail-chasing," Karen replied. "But since you have this special bond with these particular branches, I will allow you to take them the rest of the way."

"Thanks, Karen. I appreciate it."

Stick Dog gathered the branches and turned backward, preparing to grab them and drag them across the meadow.

"Karen?"

"Yes, Stick Dog?"

"Since you let me take the branches the rest

of the way," he said, "could I do something for you? You know, in return?"

"Sure."

"Great. Thanks," he said, and smiled. He nodded at Karen, then he tilted his head toward the branches. "Hop on."

And Karen—with great glee—hopped on.

Chapter 16

THE ULTIMATE SHAKE

All five dogs gathered right outside Stick Dog's pipe, forming a circle around that pile of pine tree branches.

"How do we put this tree back together?" Stripes asked.

"We don't have all the branches," Poo-Poo said.

"Or the trunk," added Karen.

Mutt had gone into the pipe briefly and was now chewing nervously on that silver high-heeled shoe again.

"We're not reassembling it *exactly*," Stick

Dog replied. "It
won't be as big,
of course. But I
don't think that will
matter to Santa
Claus. It sounded
like Christmas trees
can be any size at all. But they're all the
same shape. They're triangles. And we use
these branches like this."

Stick Dog picked up a branch and stuck
it into the snow to stand it up. The other
dogs just watched, heads tilted, as Stick Dog
demonstrated what he meant. He stood up
two more branches on either side of the
first. He leaned them together at the top.

"I get it!" Stripes yelped, eagerly picking up a pine tree branch so she could participate.

Poo-Poo and Karen did the same thing. Mutt dropped the high-heeled shoe and joined in as well.

Stick Dog stepped back and watched. He was happy that his friends understood what he had envisioned—and worked together to carry it out. It helped that the branches could lean against the hillside and the edge of Stick Dog's pipe. It also helped that they could stick the branches in the snow and stand them up that way.

In less than five minutes, their Christmas tree was assembled. They stepped back and looked at it.

Stripes spoke for the group when she yelled, "It's beautiful!"

"It most definitely is," Stick Dog said. "Now we have to decorate it."

"How do we do that?" Karen asked.

"Let's get into the pipe and warm up," Stick Dog said, leading the way. "We'll have some more beef jerky after all that hard work."

Nobody argued with that idea and they followed him inside. They were cheerful as they sat and chewed on their jerky, turning their heads often to look toward the pipe's entrance. They liked the way their shoe-stockings looked and they were proud of constructing a Christmas tree from all those branches.

"Okay," Stick Dog said after swallowing his final bite of jerky. He turned to look at his friends. "We got the stockings up. We've got a Christmas tree. But we still have to decorate it."

"How are we going to do that, Stick Dog?" Poo-Poo asked.

"We'll need to depend on Mutt," Stick Dog said.

"I'm happy to help," Mutt said immediately. "What do you need me to do?"

"Mutt," Stick Dog said, and cocked his head a smidgeon. He looked at him with great seriousness. He lowered his voice. "I need you to shake like you've never shaken before. We need everything you have stored in your fur."

Mutt took a deep inhale and nodded his head with a strong look of determination.

"Stand back, everybody," Mutt said,

spreading his legs wide. Poo-Poo, Stick Dog, Stripes, and Karen all took a step back.

And Mutt shook.

And he did just what Stick Dog requested: he shook like he never shook before.

He shook from the tip of his nose to the tip of his tail. He shook his head, shoulders, belly, and hips. He stuck one leg out at a time and shook each one individually. He shook with great energy and vigor.

Dozens of things flew out of his fur in the first twenty seconds. Then Mutt shook even harder and dozens of other things flew out from deeper and deeper parts of his fur.

After a minute and a half—and after ten seconds of nothing flying out at all—he stopped.

"Wow," Poo-Poo said, looking at all the objects scattered around Mutt. "Dude, that's a LOT of stuff!"

Mutt smiled, panting as he did.

It would be impossible to name everything that was there. Totally impossible. But just to give you a general idea, here is a list of some of the things.

A yellow mitten
Four rubber bands
Five screws
Four nails

Eight bottle caps

Three broken pencils

Two plastic forks

Two dented Ping-Pong balls

Six shoestrings

Two more candy canes

Three black markers

A blue straw

Two crumpled-up napkins

A paper cup

A pink eraser

Three chopsticks

Seven paper clips

Two toothbrushes

Four socks

A chewed-up tennis ball

Three candy bar wrappers

And loads and loads of other stuff

"Thanks, Mutt," Stick Dog said, looking

around at everything that flew out of his fur. He was, frankly, amazed that one dog could carry so much in his fur. "Poo-Poo's right. This is an impressive amount of stuff."

Mutt was quite modest, but you could tell he appreciated his friends' praise. He smiled, nodded, and picked up one of the Ping-Pong balls and said, "I haven't seen this in years."

"Would you like to hang it on the tree?" Stick Dog said. "We're going to use some of these things to decorate the Christmas tree."

"Sure!"

"Great. I think you should hang the first

decoration," Stick Dog said. "Since you provided everything. Everybody else grab a few things that you think would look good on the tree."

Poo-Poo, Karen, and Stripes were all excited about this idea. They quickly snatched some items and hustled out to the tree.

Mutt placed the dented Ping-Pong ball right in the middle of the stacked and arranged pine tree branches. And then Poo-Poo, Karen, Stripes, and Stick Dog began to place their objects too.

Now, they didn't have hooks and looped string to hang their decorations. And that meant some things fell off the tree and they had to place them again, but it was no big deal. And some things worked remarkably well—like the shoestrings and the plastic forks.

After their first round of decorating, the dogs stepped back and observed their work.

"It's coming along quite nicely," Stripes said. "But it still needs more decorations."

"Yep," Poo-Poo agreed. "Needs more stuff."

"Well, there are plenty more things inside," Stick Dog said. He looked up at the sky. It was evening now—and getting darker. The sun had set and he could see the moon rising over the treetops. It was going to be a full moon tonight.

"What about lights, Stick Dog?" Karen asked. "Lucy said Christmas trees need to have lights."

"I don't think we can do that," he answered honestly. "Those lights need to be plugged in, I think. We don't have any lights—and we don't have a place to plug them in anyway."

"That's a bummer," Poo-Poo said, a hint of distress in his voice. "What if Santa doesn't see our tree because it doesn't have lights? What if we don't get his attention? He might fly right over us."

"He might. It's true," Stick Dog said.

"We could get a giant bow and arrow!" Karen yelped excitedly. "And when he flies by on his sleigh, we'll shoot it at him. We'll aim it so it whizzes right by his ear. And he'll think, *Hey, I wonder who just shot that arrow at me.* He'll be so curious, he'll turn his reindeer around and come find Stick Dog's pipe! It's the perfect attention-getting plan!"

Stick Dog didn't mention that shooting arrows at someone is not a very nice way to get their attention. Or that, you know, you might not aim correctly and actually hit Santa Claus or one of the reindeer. Or that, umm, if you're shooting arrows at someone, they might not be in a happy, gift-giving mood.

"We don't have a giant bow and arrow,"
Stick Dog said instead. "Otherwise, we
might have been able to try your idea. But
remember what we said before. We think
Santa is a pretty smart guy. We think he'll
recognize that those shoes are really our
stockings. And that these branches are our
Christmas tree. He might know we're here
even without lights on the tree."

This was enough encouragement to change
the mood of the group, Stick Dog could tell.

"It's possible," Poo-Poo
said, and wagged his tail. "It
just might be possible!"

"All right," Stick Dog said, turning from the
pipe toward the meadow and forest. He
knew he had to get to Lucy's. "Is it okay

with you guys if you keep decorating while I
go to town to get the cookies from Lucy?"

"Sure, Stick Dog," Karen said. "Say hi to
Lucy for us. It seems like ages since we've
seen her."

"But we saw her last night," Stick Dog said.

"I know," Karen replied. "Like I said—ages."

"Okay," Stick Dog said, and smiled. "I'll tell
her."

And that's what happened.

Mutt, Karen, Stripes, and Poo-Poo
continued to decorate the tree. And Stick
Dog hurried off to see Lucy—and get some
cookies for Santa.

He crossed the meadow and entered the forest. He felt relatively confident that they had prepared for Christmas the best they could—especially having so little time. He liked the holiday season. He felt himself welling up with something. He couldn't quite put his paw on what it was—but it felt special.

The Christmas spirit maybe. And there was still one special thing about Christmas that Stick Dog didn't know.

And Lucy was going to tell him about it.

Chapter 17

WAIT!

TAP,
TAP,
SCRAAAATCH.

Tap, tap, scraaaatch.

Lucy was waiting for him. She opened the door in two seconds. She poked her head out to ensure it was Stick Dog, winked at him, and opened the door wider.

Lucy guided him to where he and his friends had been the day before—near the big silver refrigerator and the long table. The three thick rolls of aluminum foil were still on the table, but the apron and knives were gone now. There was also a small paper bag—Stick Dog thought the cookies were probably in there.

"My roommate, Mike, is asleep upstairs again," she said quietly. "Nothing to worry about."

"Great," he whispered, standing close to her.

"How did your Christmas preparations go?" Lucy asked.

"Pretty good, I think," Stick Dog answered. "We used five of Mutt's shoes for stockings and we hung them on my pipe. And we bit off a bunch of pine tree branches and stood them up in the shape of a Christmas tree. We decorated it with stuff from Mutt's fur."

"That sounds good."

"Karen was disappointed that we didn't have lights for the tree," Stick Dog said. "Do you think that matters?"

"I don't think so," Lucy said. "Although if it had lights there would probably be a better chance that Santa would see it."

"That's what I thought too," he acknowledged. "But there's not much we can do about that. Even if we had lights, I don't have electricity at my pipe anyway. We're just kind of hoping he sees the stockings and the tree. That's the only way he's going to know we live there. We haven't figured out any other way to do it."

"Santa's pretty smart. There's a decent chance he'll figure it out," Lucy said.

"That's what we're hoping too," Stick Dog said. "Although Karen did have one other idea to get his attention."

"What was that?"

"To get a giant bow and arrow and shoot it right past Santa's ear," Stick Dog answered.

He opened his eyes wide, squeezed his lips together in a smile, and nodded his head. "It's true. That's what she suggested."

"That's a very, umm, Karen thing to say," Lucy said, and laughed. She stretched up, placing her front paws on the table. She grasped the little paper bag in her mouth and dropped back down. She put it on the floor in front of Stick Dog. "Here are the cookies."

"Thanks so much, Lucy," he said. He didn't want to leave just yet, but he knew he should get back to his friends. "You've been so helpful with everything, but I think I better get back to my pipe."

"No problem," Lucy said slowly. It seemed like she had something else to say, but then stopped herself. "Be careful on the way back. It's late—and it's dark."

"There's a bright full moon tonight," Stick Dog said, turning toward the door. "So I can see pretty well. I don't think I'll bonk my head into a tree or anything."

"Like Poo-Poo would," Lucy said, and giggled.

"Right," Stick Dog said, smiled, and shook his head. He leaned his head down to pick up the cookie bag. "Like Poo-Poo would."

Lucy pulled the belt down to open the door. She poked her head out to make sure there were no humans in the alley. There weren't. She looked up at the moon.

"The coast is clear," she said, turning her head over her shoulder to look at Stick Dog. "And you're right. The moon is full and super-bright tonight."

Stick Dog stepped out into the alley with the bag in his mouth.

"Thanks again for the cookies," he mumbled.

"You're welcome," she said. "And Merry Christmas."

"Merry Christmas," Stick Dog said, and smiled. He took three steps down the alley.

But he didn't take a fourth.

"Stick Dog! Wait!" Lucy yelped quietly—but urgently. "Come back!"

Chapter 18

ONE MORE THING

Stick Dog hustled back inside. He heard the urgency in Lucy's voice. And he knew she was smart. He didn't know why she wanted him to come back, but he trusted Lucy completely.

She closed the door.

"What is it?" Stick Dog asked quickly. "Did you see a human come into the alley? I didn't see anybody."

"No, that's not it," she said, and smiled.

"Oh, good," he said, and relaxed. Lucy didn't seem worried—she seemed excited about something. "Then what is it?"

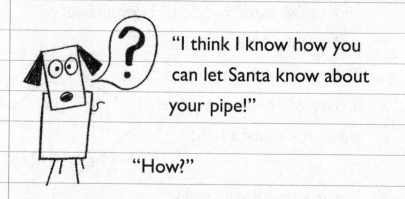

"I think I know how you can let Santa know about your pipe!"

"How?"

Lucy hustled back to the table, propped herself up again, and grabbed one of the thick rolls of aluminum foil. She came back and dropped it on the floor between them.

"I saw that earlier," Stick Dog said. He was

getting excited too. "What is it? And how will it help?"

"It's called aluminum foil," Lucy answered, and unrolled it a little bit. Then she folded a corner of it over to reveal the other side. "It's shiny! Look!"

It was shiny. Really shiny.

"The full moon," whispered Stick Dog. He was putting together what Lucy had in mind. "It could reflect the light of the full moon."

"There's a ton of it on this roll," Lucy said. "It's really thin, so a roll has hundreds of feet on it. You can lay it out in the meadow outside your pipe. You could lay it out like a big arrow."

"Pointing at my pipe!"

"Exactly!"

"It could work," Stick Dog said happily. "It could really work!"

"There's no way Santa Claus won't see a big bright arrow when he flies over tonight!" Lucy said. "You could even say Karen gave you the idea with her crazy bow-and-arrow plan."

"She would definitely like that," he said, and stepped toward Lucy. Their heads were close together. He rubbed the side of his face against Lucy's for a second, then whispered in her ear, "You are so smart. Thank you."

"You're welcome," she whispered back. They stepped away from each other. "I'm just glad we thought of something."

"Me too."

"I know you're in a hurry and everything, Stick Dog," Lucy whispered. "But I was wondering if I could tell you about one more Christmas tradition before you go. It will just take a minute. Is that okay?"

"Of course."

"I'll be right back," Lucy said, and hurried through the door to the meat store. She was back in sixteen seconds.

"I wanted to tell you about this," Lucy said,
holding out three green stems with little
white berries on them.

"What's that?"

"It's called mistletoe."

(!)

Chapter 19

FINISHED

There was a lightness in Stick Dog's step as he made his way back to his pipe. It was awkward carrying the roll of aluminum foil and the bag of cookies in his mouth. He had to be careful making his way through town, of course. And it was tougher to navigate through the woods with the roll of aluminum foil sticking out of his mouth in both directions.

But none of that bothered Stick Dog at all.

It was Christmas Eve—and he was feeling the Christmas spirit. Lucy had, ahem, taught him about mistletoe. And he had a plan—a plan that just might work—to direct Santa to his pipe.

He emerged from the forest and into the meadow outside of his pipe. The full moon provided plenty of light for him to see in this wide-open space.

Stick Dog saw their shoe-stockings hanging on his pipe. He saw their Christmas tree covered with dozens and dozens of things from Mutt's fur. He dropped the roll of aluminum foil right where he was and carried the cookies to his pipe.

He peeked inside and saw that Karen, Poo-Poo, and Stripes were gathered around Mutt—the shaggiest and warmest of their gang. They were all fast asleep.

Stick Dog smiled and watched them for a moment. He wasn't surprised they were exhausted. It had been a very busy day.

He took three chocolate chip cookies quietly from the bag. He laid the bag flat near the Christmas tree and put the cookies on top of it, thinking Santa would find them there easily.

Something about watching his friends sleeping so soundly made Stick Dog sleepy too, but he knew he had one more job to do. He hustled across the meadow. He got the aluminum foil and began to unroll it. He tried it with his front paws first, but that was awkward and slow. Then he figured out an easier—and faster—way.

He laid the aluminum foil tube down and pushed it with his nose. It usually rolled

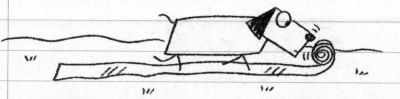

two or three feet with each push. Using this method, he rolled a long straight line from the edge of the meadow straight toward his pipe. He tore the foil there and then rolled two straight, angled lines to form the shape of an arrow.

"Not too bad," Stick Dog whispered to himself as he stepped back to look at the giant aluminum foil arrow. The moon was high in the sky and bright white. He could see its light reflected from the foil. And he suspected that looking down on the arrow from the sky would make it show up even better. "Not too bad at all."

He shivered. He'd been so busy he hadn't realized how cold he was. He was ready to get inside and get warm.

Stick Dog took one last look at their Christmas tree.

"Only thing missing is the lights," Stick Dog said, shrugged, and started to go inside.

Then he stopped.

He looked down at the roll of aluminum foil. There was still plenty left.

"If the moonlight reflects off the aluminum foil arrow," he whispered to himself, "it would also reflect off aluminum foil on the tree."

He got to work fast.

He tore about twenty small pieces of foil off the roll. He crumpled those pieces into crinkled-up balls.

And he placed them all over the tree.

He was ready to sleep—but he had to look. He had to see their Christmas tree from a distance. He went out to the middle of the meadow and turned to look at the tree.

"Lights," he said proudly. The foil balls twinkled as they reflected the moonlight. "We've got lights."

It was the last thing Stick Dog did.

He moved slowly into his pipe, dragged an

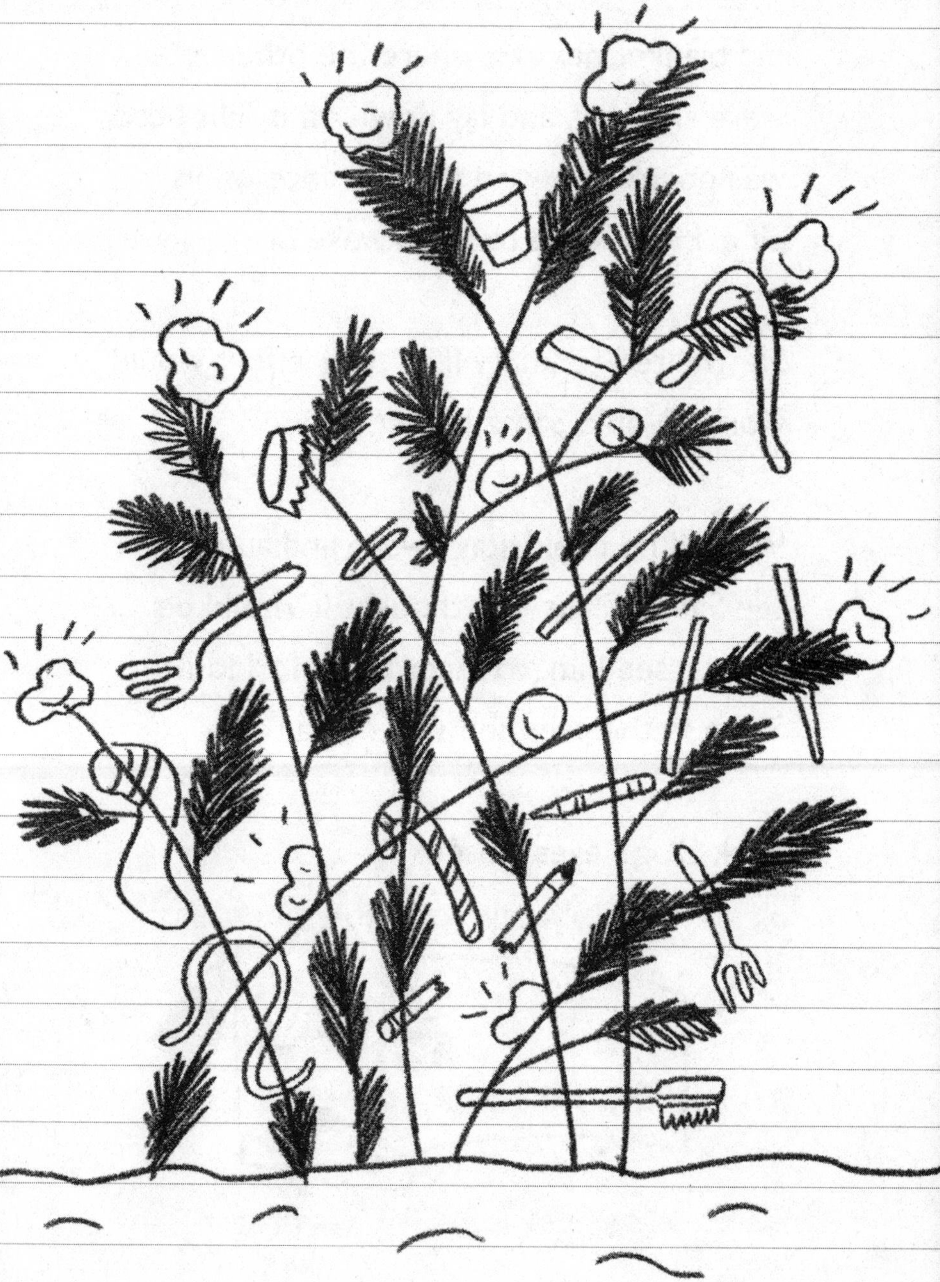

old blanket next to where the other four were sleeping, and lay down on it. His head was pointed toward the entrance of his pipe. He wanted to stay awake.

He wanted to know if all their effort would work. Would Santa come?

What if he could stay awake and actually see Santa Claus? He thought it would be nice to see him, to meet him. He'd look Santa in the eyes and wag his tail.

Stick Dog's eyes closed.

And when they opened next he was looking
someone in the eyes.

But it wasn't Santa Claus.

Chapter 20
CHRISTMAS MORNING

When Stick Dog opened his eyes for the first time on Christmas morning, Karen was staring right at him. They were only two inches apart.

"Wake up, sleepyhead! It's Christmas!" Karen yelled and jumped up as high as she could—almost six inches—three times in a row. She called to Mutt, Stripes, and Poo-Poo. "Stick Dog's awake, everybody! We can go look now!"

Stripes, Mutt, and Poo-Poo all yelped happily.

"How long have you guys been up?" Stick Dog asked, pushing himself up to all fours.

"We've been waiting for you forever!" Poo-Poo exclaimed. "It's been, like, three minutes! Maybe four!"

Stick Dog was, of course, happy to see his friends so excited. But he had been up much later than them—and he'd been busy. He rubbed his eyes and shook his head a little.

"Do you think Santa came?!" Stripes yelped. "Do you? Do you?! Do you??!!"

Mutt was chewing nervously—happily, but nervously—on an old gray sneaker.

"Well," Stick Dog said, stretching one more time. "There's only one way to find out."

That's all Poo-Poo, Stripes, Karen, and Mutt needed to hear. They raced out of the pipe. They got outside in three seconds. They skidded, stopped, turned, and sprinted up the hillside to get their shoe-stockings. Stick Dog trailed closely behind.

They jerked to a stop before each of their shoe-stockings, staring in disbelief. There was a big rawhide bone sticking out of four of the

shoes—Stick Dog's, Karen's, Stripes's, and Poo-Poo's.

Something different stuck out of Mutt's.

"I can't believe it!" Mutt whispered. There was a brand-new, high-topped, leather basketball sneaker shoved halfway into Mutt's work boot stocking.

"There's a shoe in my shoe!"

They retrieved their delicious gifts and hurried down the snowy hillside to the Christmas tree.

There was a big box with a red ribbon sitting next to the tree. There was a label on the box.

"To five good dogs," Stick Dog read out loud. "From Santa."

"Open it, Stick Dog!" Karen screamed with delight.

Stick Dog lifted the lid slowly off the big box. They could not tell what was inside the box immediately. Tissue paper covered its contents. A single piece of paper was on top of the tissue paper.

"There's a note," Stick Dog said, lifting the piece of paper out of the box.

"What's it say?!" asked Stripes, hopping up and down.

"'I have a few extra of these,'" Stick Dog read. "'They're all yours. Merry Christmas! Santa.'"

I have a few
extra of these.
They're all
yours.
Merry
Christmas!
—Santa

Poo-Poo, Mutt, Karen, and Stripes stared down into the box as Stick Dog pulled the tissue paper aside to reveal what was inside.

There were hundreds and hundreds of Christmas cookies.

THE END.

Tom Watson lives in Chicago with his wife, daughter, and son. He also has a dog, as you could probably guess. The dog is a Labrador-Newfoundland mix. Tom says he looks like a Labrador with a bad perm. He wanted to name the dog "Put Your Shirt On" (please don't ask why), but he was outvoted by his family. The dog's name is Shadow. Early in his career Tom worked in politics, including a stint as the chief speechwriter for the governor of Ohio. This experience helped him develop the unique storytelling narrative style of the Stick Dog, Stick Cat, and Trouble at Table 5 books. Tom's time in politics also made him realize a very important thing: kids are way smarter than adults. And it's a lot more fun and rewarding to write stories for them than to write speeches for grown-ups.

Visit www.stickdogbooks.com

for more fun stuff.

Also available as an ebook.

STICK WITH READING!

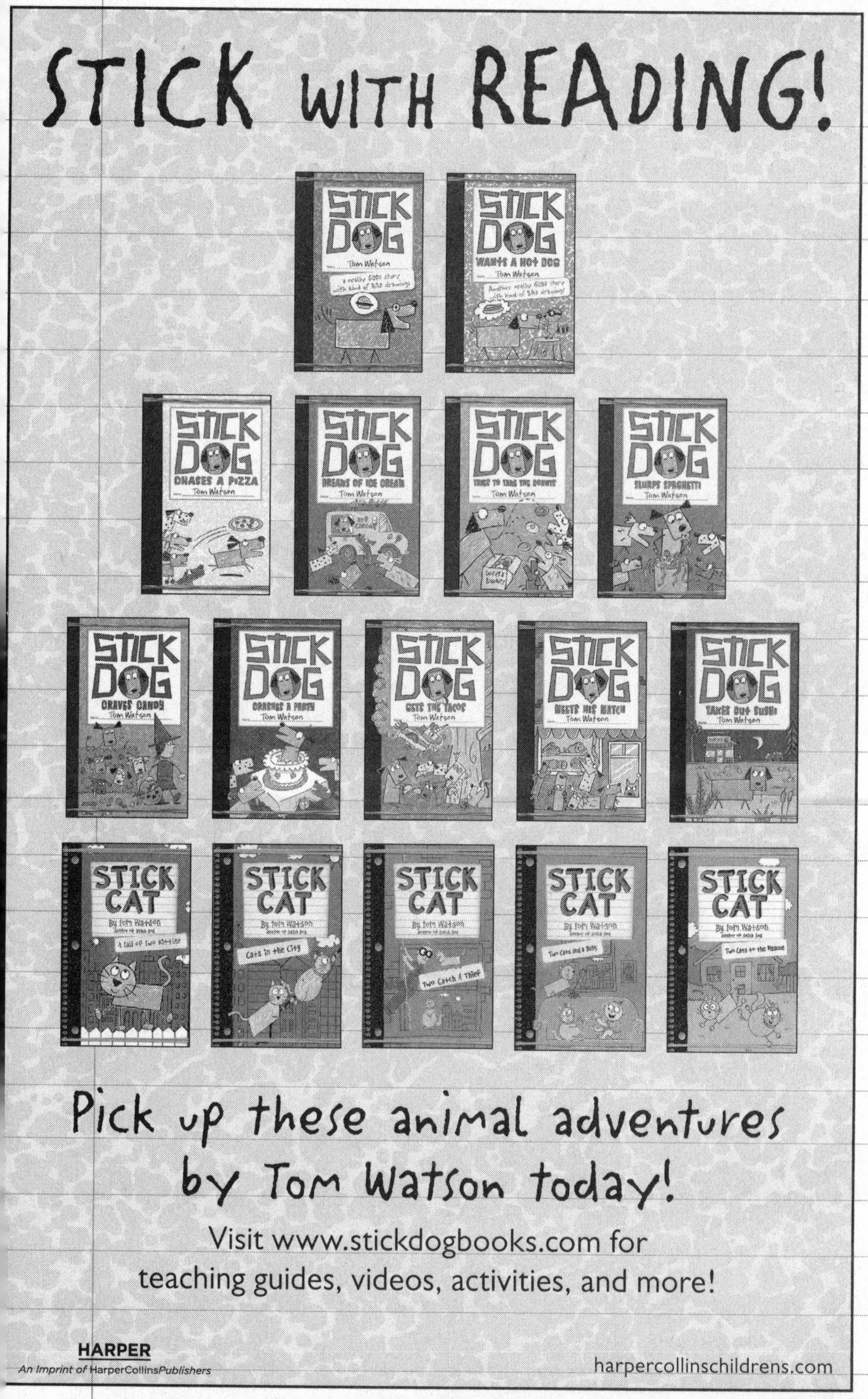
STICK DOG
Tom Watson
A really GOOD story with kind of BAD drawings
STICK DOG
WANTS A HOT DOG
Tom Watson
Another really GOOD story with kind of BAD drawings
STICK DOG
CHASES A PIZZA
Tom Watson
STICK DOG
DREAMS OF ICE CREAM
Tom Watson
STICK DOG
TRIES TO TAKE THE DONUTS
Tom Watson
STICK DOG
SLURPS SPAGHETTI
Tom Watson
STICK DOG
CRAVES CANDY
Tom Watson
STICK DOG
CRASHES A PARTY
Tom Watson
STICK DOG
GETS THE TACOS
Tom Watson
STICK DOG
MEETS HIS MATCH
Tom Watson
STICK DOG
TAKES OUT SUSHI
Tom Watson
STICK CAT
By Tom Watson
A Tail of Two Kitties
STICK CAT
By Tom Watson
Cats in the City
STICK CAT
By Tom Watson
Two Catch a Thief
STICK CAT
By Tom Watson
Two Cats and a Baby
STICK CAT
By Tom Watson
Two Cats to the Rescue

Pick up these animal adventures by Tom Watson today!

Visit www.stickdogbooks.com for
teaching guides, videos, activities, and more!

HARPER
An Imprint of HarperCollinsPublishers

harpercollinschildrens.com